Untried Heart

Nicky Charles
&
Jan Gordon

ACKNOWLEDGEMENTS

We'd like to thank our wonderful Beta readers…
Carmen
Kalia
Leila
Lorna
Norma
Suzi
Your input was invaluable!

This book is written in memory of

Deborah Davidson

She is our very own angel with teal coloured wings.
Deborah will be forever remembered for her love of
animals,
her kind and generous spirit,
and for the courage with which she battled ovarian cancer.

Fly free, dear friend

Prologue

England, December 1923...

"We'll be leaving in half an hour, Eugenie. Will you be ready?"

"Yes, of course." Eugenie nodded at the raven-haired girl who popped her head into the office. "I'll meet you near the side entrance, Annabelle."

Annabelle waved and breezed away down the hallway while Eugenie returned her attention to the tiny window of the spartan office in which she worked.

She shivered. The small fire in the grate barely made any impression on the arctic temperature in the room. God only knew how condensation could form on the glass. The newspaper had said it was the coldest December in decades so probably it was warmer inside than she thought it was. She rubbed her fingers over the pane to clear it in order to see outside. A wide smile brightened her face at the sight that greeted her.

The smile was unusual, not that she was by nature a somber individual, but her workplace seldom inspired anything close to a cheery expression. Surrounded by floor-to-ceiling shelves that housed the dusty tomes her father used for research and seated by a desk covered in bits of paper bearing his almost indecipherable scrawl, the atmosphere was decidedly dull and dry, more likely to induce a frown than signs of happiness. But today…today was different.

To start with, it was snowing—again. Big fluffy flakes of the purest white drifted down, gathering in the corners on the window ledge, clinging to the bare branches of the trees and covering the courtyard in a sparkling white blanket. No doubt many were complaining about the roads becoming slippery, although snow was better than ice, but she didn't care. In her mind, the wonder of this weather meant there would be a white Christmas and that was something to be celebrated. If she were a daring sort, she'd slip outside and dance in the snow, perhaps attempt making a snow angel or even a snowman. Of course, she wasn't the daring sort and she had a large stack of work to complete before her father returned from his lecturing tour in two days.

That tour was another reason for her smile. Her parents weren't home and she'd had the house to herself for an entire week, if one didn't include the hired help. She'd been able to lounge on the sofa and read a novel after dinner rather than an academic paper, and had drunk hot chocolate before bed without being warned of the inadvisability of such an action. At twenty-five years of age, she was a spinster, living at home with her parents and still following their dictates just as she had when she was six years old. The simple freedoms of the past few days were a heady experience compared to her usual life.

And tonight…well, tonight was going to be truly amazing. A few of the other girls working in the university offices had invited her to go to dinner and then on to a small art show. She didn't often socialize with the other women who worked at the university beyond brief comments about the weather. Usually she travelled to and from work with her father, his stern expression enough to scare off any potential friends…or suitors. But in his absence, she'd struck up a conversation with a few of the girls and they'd eagerly invited her to join them for lunch the other day and now for an evening of adventure.

The clock on the mantel chimed and she gave a start. It was almost time to leave and she hadn't done the work she'd planned on completing, but tonight she dared not stay late. Instead, she gathered her papers into a neat pile and made the fire safe before putting on her coat and leaving the room, making sure she latched the door carefully behind her. Feeling lighter than she had in what seemed like ages, she hurried down the corridor.

Several hours later she was laughing with her new friends as they, wrapped in thick woollen scarves and hats, made their way to a small shop front that served as both an art gallery and a studio. It was owned by Jonathan, Annabelle's brother. He was an artist and apparently, quite bohemian.

"He told me to bring as many of my friends as possible," Annabelle explained as she pushed open the door. "He's just starting out and hopes to find a wealthy patron."

They entered the building, snowflakes swirling into the room with them and giggled as they pushed the door shut, blocking out the brisk winter breeze. A man came hurrying over, his blond hair over-long and his shirt unbuttoned at the throat, the opening filled with a colourful and flamboyant cravat.

"Annie!" He grabbed Annabelle by the waist and twirled her about.

Eugenie watched in wonder and envy at the warmth in the man's gaze. She had no siblings, no one who rushed across a room to greet her, no one who would grab her by the waist and twirl her around. At best, her father gave her a nod while her mother delivered a very cool kiss to the air near her cheek.

"Jonathan, put me down!" Annabelle—Annie—was laughing.

"You brought the usual crowd, I see." Jonathan let Annie go and turned to smile at the others who greeted him with familiarity, obviously having met him before. His eyes skimmed over the group and then paused on Eugenie. "But here's someone new."

The others parted as Jonathan stepped forward, hand extended. Annie paused in the middle of removing her coat and glanced at Jonathan. Eugenie, suddenly very conscious of her dowdy clothes, felt even more shy and awkward than she normally did around men. The other girls had all changed into gorgeous cocktail dresses before leaving work, their short hemlines acceptable now in this new age of jazz and freedom, whereas just a few short years ago their appearance would have been considered terribly shocking. Unfortunately, due to her parents' strict rules, all she had to wear was a serviceable tweed skirt and a smart silk blouse, her only adornment a single string of pearls.

"Yes, this is Eugenie Winslow. Eugenie, this is my rascal of a brother, Jonathan."

Jonathan took her hand and Eugenie gave a shy smile, feeling her cheeks heat up under his steady gaze.

"I'm delighted to meet you, Eugenie."

"Come along, everyone. Coats off." Annabelle began to organize the group. Jonathan released Eugenie's hand and led them into the room, offering introductions to those gathered. Eugenie followed, flexing her fingers that still tingled from Jonathan's touch.

It was a diverse crowd; old, young, a few obviously well-off individuals but most were middle-class and the rest students from the university. Animated conversations took place as people debated the worth of Jonathan's paintings that hung around the room while others argued politics or the merits of a play they'd recently seen.

Eugenie hung back, not sure how to act in such a crowd. It was a far cry from the staid gatherings her parents held that were more geared to impressing others and climbing the social ladder of academia. Those evenings were tediously boring and she often found herself cornered by elderly colleagues of her father, listening to them tout their latest work on dead languages. While they were quite likely enjoying themselves, she often wanted to scream and run from the room. However, being the well-trained and dutiful daughter that she was, she nodded and smiled while the spark of life in her was quashed more and more with each passing year.

Someone was playing some jazz or maybe it was blues – she never could understand the difference – on an old upright piano in the corner. Impulsively, she began to tap her foot in time to the beat, smiling faintly as she watched a few of the others start to dance. What must it be like to feel such a sense of freedom?

"Eugenie, right?"

A voice beside her caused her to jump.

"Sorry, I didn't mean to startle you." It was Jonathan.

"You didn't startle me. Well, you did, but it's all right." She stumbled over her response.

He smiled, his eyes crinkling in the corners. "You have an amazing profile. Have you ever been painted?"

"Painted? Er…no."

"Would you like to be? I'd love to try to capture your smile." Even as he spoke, Jonathan was taking her arm and leading her towards the rear of the room.

"I don't… I mean, I'm not sure…" Her mind was in a muddle, the warmth of his touch on her arm, his closeness; it was all quite new to her.

"Nothing improper, of course," Jonathan assured as he drew back a curtain revealing a small studio. "Just sit here. The others can watch."

"But…"

He pulled out a chair and urged her to sit, ignoring her protests. "It won't take long, I promise."

She sat and watched as he pulled an easel away from the wall and placed a canvas on it.

"Anyone want to watch a genius at work?" He called out to those gathered while he squirted paint on a palette and picked out a brush.

A few wandered over, good naturedly ribbing him with comments of "Where's the genius?" and "What? You're actually going to work?"

Annabelle appeared, cigarette holder in one hand and a cocktail in the other, and grinned. "Oh, this will be so exciting. Just think, Eugenie, your portrait might end up in a major gallery someday for everyone to see!"

The very idea made her stomach do a flip-flop. If her parents ever knew she'd sat for a painting in a place such as this... She moved to rise but Jonathan was there, moving her head, turning her shoulders.

"Your hair..." He frowned.

"What?" She reached up wondering if the wind had caught it but he brushed her hands away.

"It's too severe. Let me soften it a bit." Jonathan began to fuss with her hair, removing pins and loosening tendrils so they fell about her face. "There. That's much better." He leaned close to her ear. "I really dislike the short bobs the women are wearing now. Long tresses give a sense of mystery and sensual romance that appeal to my artist's soul. But don't tell Annie."

"I won't." She could feel her face warming as his breath caressed her ear and her heart beat faster.

"Hold this pose, please."

His touch once again befuddled her as he angled her chin and so she stayed where she was, watching him work, enjoying the attention he was paying her, the flattering comments about the colour of her eyes, the shape of her nose... It was a heady experience and while she was sure a worldly man like Jonathan had no real interest in her, it was thrilling nonetheless. And, hadn't she been wanting to have an adventure, to do something different? Surely, this had to qualify!

How long she held the pose, she wasn't sure, but when Jonathan finally declared he had done all he could in one sitting, she was decidedly stiff.

"Here, let me help you." Jonathan took her hand as she stood and must have noticed her wincing for he began to massage her shoulders. "Sorry, I kept you longer than I should have but the painting is amazing. Come."

He led her to the easel and she gave a soft gasp.

"That can't be me!"

Jonathan laughed. "It's no where near completed yet, but it most certainly is you. I'll spend some more time on it over the coming days."

She examined the painting carefully. It *was* her; her nose, her hair, her eyes, but she looked different somehow. Her eyes sparkled, her skin glowed. The mousy brown of her hair showed gold and red highlights.

"Let us see!" The others pushed their way in, all exclaiming over the painting and congratulating Jonathan on his skill. Someone gave Eugenie a glass of an exotic drink and she sipped it, allowing the warmth to seep into her as she basked in the praise that swirled around her.

All too soon, Annabelle was saying it was time to go since they all had to work the next day. Coats were donned and goodbyes called out. Jonathan came over and hugged Annabelle. Then, much to her surprise, he hugged Eugenie, too, even giving her a brief peck on the cheek. Eugenie felt her breath catch in her chest and was still in a daze as the others led her out of the building.

The kiss hadn't meant anything, she was sure of it, but it *had* been her first kiss. Surreptitiously, she touched her cheek, still able to feel the soft brush of his lips, the faint rasp of the stubble on his chin.

That night, she fell asleep dreaming of a certain golden-haired artist.

The next morning, she made her way to work floating on a bubble of happiness. The snow had stopped during the night but the temperature had plummeted even further. Underfoot, the ground was icy and she planted her feet carefully as she walked to avoid slipping. Tomorrow was Christmas Eve and the world sparkled in the cold sunshine. Life was wonderful, exciting, amazing…

"Eugenie, wait!"

She looked around and saw Annabelle hurrying towards her. The girl skidded to a halt beside her, laughing, her cheeks pink from the cold.

"I'm glad I caught up with you. Wasn't last night simply the cat's meow?"

"Yes, it was." Eugenie smiled at the slang as Annabelle linked arms with her. She'd never really had a friend before.

"I'm so glad you came with us. Next Friday we're planning on going to the theatre. Will you come?"

She hesitated to reply. Her parents would be back by then. "I'll let you know."

"Okay." Annabelle gave a little hop as she avoided an uneven paving stone. "Jonathan came by my house last night on his way home. He was really pleased with the painting and hopes you'll come back for another sitting so he can finish it."

Jonathan had asked about her? Excitement filled her at the idea he might really be interested in her.

Annabelle continued talking. "He said, if you have time, tomorrow would be perfect. His wife will keep the baby out of the way and—"

Eugenie felt as if she'd been punched in the stomach. "His wife?"

"You didn't meet her last night. She took my niece over to my parents' place since she knows how boisterous Jonathan's art shows can get."

Jonathan was married.

With a child.

The news had her stunned.

The gloom of the day suddenly became apparent to her. The icy wind, the coldness of the ground creeping through her boots and making her toes ache.

"Eugenie, are you all right? You look very pale." Annabelle stared at her in concern.

"I'm fine. I just..." She shook her head, not knowing what to say. There was a hurt building inside her heart and she wanted to curl up somewhere to nurse the pain. No man had ever paid attention to her before and she'd misread Jonathan's intentions completely. Had the others realized? Did Annabelle know and was that why she'd mentioned his wife? Mortified, she didn't dare look at the other girl's face in case it was filled with pity.

It was the sound of crying that finally drew her from her introspection. A mother and child were walking just ahead of her, the child pulling to get away and pointing towards the road while the mother hurried along, her shoulders hunched against the bitter wind. Eugenie looked towards where the little boy was pointing and noticed a stuffed bear lying in the gutter. The little one must have dropped it but the mother hadn't noticed.

"Wait!" Not thinking, she acted instinctively, calling out and hurrying to pick up the toy. In her haste, her foot slipped on the ice and she gave a cry as she felt herself falling. Out of the corner of her eye, she saw a lumbering delivery truck approaching and tried to twist out of the way. Her head hit the curb and pain exploded through her body. Annabelle's scream was the last sound she heard before darkness encased her.

Chapter 1

Present day...

If there was one major perk to being an angel, then it was the ability to sample any country, any weather, any experience one desired. That was what she, Eugenie Winslow, novice guardian angel, was currently doing and thoroughly loving it. In fact, it was part of her training. New guardian angels were encouraged to visit different countries and societies so as to better understand the varying nuances of the world's population. There was only one proviso…no interaction with humans.

That proviso wasn't going to be an issue for her as there was no one around for miles. Today, she was exploring the Canadian countryside, marvelling at the vast, sweeping landscape and cold, wintery weather. She'd always adored snow despite dying during the aftermath of a blizzard back in the 1920s. Right now, she was bundled up in a somewhat cumbersome man's overcoat and scarf, catching snowflakes on her tongue like a small child.

The overly large coat was a necessity because she hadn't yet mastered the trick of retracting her wings completely. She was almost there, but the tips stubbornly refused to retreat beneath her wing flaps. As well as the necessity to hide her feathered accoutrements, she needed the extra-large garment to cover the many layers of clothing she was wearing. She was definitely not used to these kinds of temperatures. At least, not yet. Apparently, guardian angels did eventually become inured to all extremes of temperature, but as she'd only been one for a few months she was still susceptible to the cold.

On entering a field, she noticed the snow was undisturbed and couldn't resist lying down to make a snow angel. As she moved her arms and legs in the requisite pattern, she quietly giggled to herself.

"A real angel making a snow angel, how silly is that?" Her voice broke the silence, echoing over the barren fields. "Almost as ridiculous as talking to myself!"

She grinned, unrepentant. In her former life, she'd never have dared to engage in such an activity but now there were no restraints on her or at least none with regards to proper behaviour in the snow!

After clambering to her feet, she brushed the wet crystals from her clothing and then assessed her snow angel. Not bad. Not bad at all. Finding a stick, she signed her name in the snow then tipped her head back to stare up at the sky. A kaleidoscope of delicate flakes drifted down in a mesmerizing swirl, catching on her lashes and tickling her cheeks before melting into cold droplets. Snow truly was amazing but very cold. She shivered as melting snow drifted inside her collar.

Just as she was thinking she'd enough experience of a Canadian winter for one day, she became aware of a change in the atmosphere. Her angelic radar on alert, she cocked her head trying to determine the source of her disquiet.

Someone was in trouble nearby, but where? She turned in a slow circle, pausing when she heard a dog barking. Was the animal trying to signal for help or was the barking a mere coincidence?

She'd had no interaction seminars yet, but she'd overheard other GAs talking about their *angelic senses*. Not having had the training, she wasn't quite sure what they'd meant but perhaps it was like when a creature goes blind their other senses become stronger or, at least, more sensitized. Trusting her instinct, she closed her eyes and stood very still listening to her inner voice. It wasn't a sound so much as a feeling that led her towards a river hidden beyond the field where there was a slight dip in the terrain.

A dog ran towards her, barking and then darting away before dashing back to her again. At first, she was startled, even a bit frightened, having had little experience with animals but then realized the creature was trying to get her to follow it.

"Is someone hurt?"

Glancing around, she saw nothing that would warrant the animal's frenetic actions but she set off after the creature anyway.

Soon she saw it run over a rickety wooden bridge spanning the water. Even as she stepped on the structure, it creaked and she froze in place not sure it would support her weight. That was when she noticed evidence of footprints, partially covered with snow and several broken boards.

"Oh no!" Ignoring her misgivings about the bridge's strength, she hurried across. The dog had disappeared from view but she could hear it barking somewhere beneath the structure. Slipping and sliding down the snowy bank, she made her way to the river's edge and that was when she saw the body.

A man was lying on the rocky bank, face down, legs still submerged in the icy water. He wasn't moving, the bit of his face that she could see appeared grey and snow was beginning to cover him. Was he alive?

Her heart pounded heavily as she knelt down and felt for a pulse on his neck. There was one, faint but definitely present. That fact sent a wave of relief washing over her.

"Out of the way, boy." The dog was prancing about, whining and pawing at the man. She shouldered the creature to the side and rolled the man over, noting there was a bloody lump on his forehead. He must have been crossing the bridge when the boards broke and he'd fallen through, hitting his head in the process.

"Sir? Can you hear me?"

There was no response.

Running her hands over the man's limbs, she detected no obvious signs of a break. It would seem the lump on his head was the main injury.

What to do?

She wasn't a healing angel; most of them worked for the archangel Raphael but there were some among the GAs. At the moment, she wished she were part of that elite group. Working as an archivist for years before applying for guardian angel status hadn't given her much experience in helping sick or injured people. All she knew was she had to get him out of the water and warm.

Gently, she tapped his cheek. "Sir? Sir? I need to move you. Can you hear me? Help a bit?"

He made not a sound, nor did his eyelids even flicker. There'd be no aid from that quarter.

"Okay, I guess this is up to me." Planting her feet as firmly as she could in the muddy slush, she gripped him under the arms and tugged.

Her eyes widened. Goodness, he was heavy! He'd barely moved at all. Taking a deep breath, she tightened her grip and tried again. This time, she was more successful and she managed to transport him a few inches. It wasn't far but at least it was encouraging.

Several more pulls and she was feeling hot and sweaty. Her arms and back were aching from the strain and her clothes were covered in mud as she scrambled to keep her footing on the slick bank. Still, she'd managed to move him enough that he was almost out of the water which was a good thing as her strength was waning. With success in sight, she adjusted her stance and gave one more mighty pull.

That one action caused several things to happen in rapid succession.

The man slid out of the water.

Her feet slipped on the bank causing a cry of surprise to escape her, and she fell backwards landing hard on her rear end, the man's head ending up in her lap.

The dog, obviously ecstatic at her success in removing the man from the water, began to bestow slobbery wet kisses to her face.

"Ugh!"

Fending off the dog, she stared at the man in her lap. The jarring of her fall must have left her dazed because for a moment all she could do was admire him.

He was a gorgeous specimen of the male of the species with strong features and thick, brown hair. His lower lip was slightly fuller than the upper, his lashes fanned out along his cheeks and she wondered what colour his eyes might be. A quick glance along the length of him gave her the impression he was tall and well-muscled.

The yipping and nuzzling of the dog reminded her this was not the time to be assessing the man's physical attributes.

"It's okay, dog. He'll be fine." She ruffled the animal's ears offering reassurance despite her own doubts about the man's well-being. "We just need to warm him up."

Beginning to remove her coat with the plan of wrapping it around him, she paused. Her clothing beneath had slits for her wing tips and she knew they'd be visible without the coat. Did she dare risk being discovered? A quick look around showed her there was no one nearby. Closing her eyes, she listened carefully.

The silence was total.

Positive there wasn't another living soul for miles, she continued to undo the buttons with trembling fingers, then took off her coat and draped it over the man. It was some help but unlikely to be enough to counteract the chilling effect of wet clothing. What else? Start a fire? No. Any wood she might find would be wet.

She bit her lip, an idea occurring to her, but it increased the risk she'd be discovered. However, she couldn't sit here and do nothing. With a decisive nod of her head, she spread her wings out to cover herself and the injured man, creating a protective dome over them both.

There was an unexpected intimacy to the position, her sitting with his head resting on her thigh. She reached out to brush the damp hair from his face and her fingers lingered on his skin, trailing over his cheek bone to his jaw, noting the roughness of stubble. An unusual sensation shot up her arm and she pulled away, curling her fingers into her palm.

How odd! It was almost like an electric charge had been exchanged between them. Vague memories of a similar sensation came to mind and she pressed her lips together as a hazy image of the painter, Jonathan, came to mind. What had ever become of him? She really had no idea. As an angel, she had no access to knowledge of a human's fate unless it was on a *need to know* basis. And right now, all she needed to know was the condition of the man she was attempting to rescue.

One thing was certain. He'd been drinking spirits. Now that they were in such close quarters, the scent of stale alcohol wafted off him causing her to wrinkle her nose and draw away with a frown. Drinking in excess was not something she admired. Mind you, he lacked the dissipated appearance one might associate with a habitual drunkard. Perhaps he'd only been having a celebratory glass or two. She gave her head a shake, realizing she was being judgemental. It didn't matter why he'd been imbibing. Her only concern should be his present well-being.

The area inside the shelter of her wings had begun to warm. Her lower limbs, pressed to the frozen ground, weren't quite so lucky and she wiggled her toes trying to ward off the iciness that was invading her feet and legs. Perhaps sensing her discomfort, the dog wiggled under the edge of her feathers and laid down near her, pressing against her side and sharing its body heat.

"Good dog." She absentmindedly patted its head while watching her charge.

Time passed. The man's colouring slowly improved, his skin feeling warmer to the touch.

"Sir? Can you hear me? It's time to wake up now." She shook his shoulder but her prompting had no more effect now than it did earlier. He was still unconscious.

She considered her options. If she left him in the snow he would, once again, be in danger from the cold. The area was isolated and she doubted he would be found before he became dangerously ill. Was there a house nearby? The man had to have come from somewhere.

Gingerly, she folded her wings back a bit so she could look around. The dog stood up and shook its fur, then nuzzled the man with its nose. Its tail gave a wag. Perhaps the animal sensed the man was improving.

"Is this man your master, dog? Were you out for a walk together? Where's home?"

Of course, the creature couldn't answer but it did cock its head and give a woof.

"Home? Is that a word you know? Where is home?"

The dog looked over its shoulder and she followed the direction of its gaze. Sure enough, in the distance she could make out a small building, its presence partly obscured by the falling snow. Well, whether it was actually the man's home or not, it would provide shelter from the weather. She just needed to get him there.

This situation was testing her ingenuity to the extreme. To all intents and purposes, she was a fledgling guardian angel, rather like a baby bird only now learning to fly. In the few weeks since Michael had accepted her into the squadron, she'd had minimal training; most of her time being spent on memorizing the rule book. When she returned to Heaven, she'd definitely have to ask for some extra instruction. But, as to the matter at hand, well, she couldn't carry the man nor fly him to shelter.

Protecting them with her wings once again, she sat and worried at her bottom lip while trying to think of a way to move him what seemed like an unsurmountable distance. She knew she was stronger than she had been as a human, but even with that extra strength she didn't think she could drag him by the feet or arms for the distance needed. Just look at how difficult it had been getting him out of the water!

If only she had a sled. There were the broken boards from the bridge but no way to hook them together. Plus, the wood was rotted and would likely disintegrate before she moved the man any distance. She tucked the edges of the huge winter coat more closely around her charge as she considered other possibilities. All she had was a dilapidated bridge, snow, a dog and... She fingered the cloth. It was a heavy woollen weave. Perhaps...

Before she started to second guess her decision, she folded her wings, pulled the coat off the man and spread it out on the snow then rolled him onto it so he was lying on his back. Quickly, she tied the arms around his chest and then grabbed the collar of the coat and began to pull it in the direction of the building she'd seen.

"I pulled him out of the water, so I should be able to do this, right dog?"

The dog watched for a minute and then, having determined the rules of this new game, grabbed the edge of the coat and began to help pull.

"Thanks, boy." She panted the words. As she'd expected, walking backwards and dragging a heavy burden was no easy feat. Her arms and legs trembling from the effort, she sat down heavily in the snow.

"At this rate, it will be dark before we get him to shelter," she told the dog. It, too, was panting, as tired as she was, and leaning against her leg. Idly, she stroked his silky head.

They were still alone, not a sound penetrating the snowy landscape besides their laboured breathing. What if she used her wings? Lift helped her fly, would it help her rescue this man? Lighten the load? It was worth a try. With a tired sigh, she pushed to her feet.

She loved her wings and, as she unfurled them, she noticed they were almost as white as the snow around her. Taking hold of the makeshift sled, she gave an experimental flap and rose an inch or two off the ground and moved towards the distant building.

The dog gave a bark of surprise then backed away whining in confusion, its feet prancing in the snow.

"It's okay, dog. It's still me." She eyed the animal nervously. Hopefully, it didn't think she was some new, large bird to chase!

After an experimental sniff, the dog settled and she began to attend to her task.

Keeping herself just off the snowy surface proved difficult but not impossible. It took only a minute or two to get the hang of it and soon she was comfortably dragging her burden, quickly arriving at the building she'd seen earlier.

From the river, she'd thought the building was a barn, but when she set the man down and opened the huge doors, it turned out there was a workshop inside. It looked like someone used the space to make furniture which was a good thing as there was a lounging chair on which she was able to set the man. He mumbled something, his eyelids flickering and she exhaled in relief. He was finally coming around.

Outside, the dog was barking and, through the window, she could see it racing towards a house on the other side of a row of trees. Uh-oh. What if someone was home and came out to investigate? She couldn't chance being discovered.

In a swirl of activity, she grabbed her coat and raced towards the door, exclaiming softly as her wing tips caught on a piece of wood. Giving an irritated tug, she freed herself, exited the building and slipped around the corner of the barn so she was hidden from the view of the house.

With a concentrated thought, she was back in Heaven, breathing a sigh of relief. She wasn't allowed to interact with humans on a conscious level yet and she hoped Michael, an archangel and her boss, never found out what had happened.

Ben groaned and lifted his hand to his throbbing head. His fingers encountered a bump and he winced as he explored the knot. What had happened? The last thing he recalled was going for a walk after downing enough whisky to dull the pain caused by his recent losses. He'd set out with the dog and then... Hadn't a board on the bridge given way? He vaguely recalled cursing just before landing in the icy water.

Looking around, he realized he was in his workshop. The door was open and snow was blowing inside. He must have dragged himself home though he had no memory of doing so.

Slowly, he stood up, weaving on unsteady legs. His clothing was soaking wet and he needed to get dried off. About to make his way to the house, something white fluttering in the wind, caught his eye.

Feathers? How did they get in here?

He plucked them free and, rubbing them between his fingers, noted their silky-smooth feel. They didn't look like anything from any bird he'd ever seen. Something niggled at the edges of his memory. Images of an angel leaning over him, stroking his face while snow drifted down around him.

Nah. It couldn't be.

He shook his head and then swore as the action caused him to wince in pain. Aspirin. That's what he needed. And a hot shower, dry clothes and then some more whisky.

Chapter 2

One year later...

"Hi, Eugenie!"

Eugenie looked up from the file she'd been studying and smiled at the angel who was passing by.

"Hello, Charlotte. It's a lovely day, isn't it?"

"Yes, but then, isn't it always?" Charlotte gave a light laugh and stopped to caress the petals of a velvety rose.

Charlotte was correct. Every day was lovely, the temperature never too hot or too cool, the sun always shining, the flowers always blooming at the peak of their beauty. Topiary trees dotted the landscape surrounded by lush gardens and sweeping lawns that were immaculately groomed. Raked gravel pathways wound between flowerbeds that never needed weeding while water fountains tinkled soothingly. Even the bench Eugenie sat on was neither too hard nor too soft.

"Yes." She smiled while thinking that, just a year ago, the perfection had been a source of irritation. It wasn't that she hadn't been grateful. She'd known she was lucky to be in Heaven rather than the *other place*. It was just that everything had been too beautiful and too perfect and too calm and... too boring. Just like her life had been back on earth.

Upon arriving in Heaven after striking her head on the curb, she'd struggled to find her place. She'd been assured nothing was expected of her but after experimenting with flying, materializing and dematerializing, and trying on various halos and styles of robes, she'd found herself longing for something to do.

There was a bulletin board with lists of jobs and she'd tried several of them from helping to prepare parties to rainbow management, but none had seemed right. In fact, most had felt trivial in the extreme. Surely, being an angel should mean more than that? Even working in the archives—the job she was most suited for due to her work with her father—hadn't appeased the restlessness within her.

In near desperation, she'd applied to join the league of guardian angels. It was practically unheard of for a fledgling angel to become a GA—most were born to the position—but she'd taken the chance anyway. Her interview with Michael, the archangel in charge of the GAs, had been a complete disaster…

Michael's office was impressive. A glass and chrome desk, dark leather furniture, a bold abstract painting on the wall; it was more like that of a CEO for a huge business empire than what one would expect of an angel. There were no puffy clouds or marble columns, no scrolls or quills for writing. As she took her seat in front of him, she decided whoever made up those illustrations of Heaven for picture books was way off base.

The man himself was equally impressive. Dark, knowing eyes, a firm, no-nonsense mouth and broad shoulders. When he looked at her, she found herself sinking down in her chair as she'd used to do when her parents had reprimanded her for being too talkative during dinner or not chewing her food enough.

"I was surprised to get your application, Miss Winslow." He flicked a glance over her, his tone causing her to swallow hard.

When he shifted his gaze back to her application form, she took a deep breath and forced herself to sit up straighter. Cowering in her chair wasn't going to help her cause. If she wanted to be a guardian angel, she needed to look the part.

"I see you've been in Heaven for some time now." Michael flipped a page over slowly.

"Since I died in 1923."

"And in the time since you've tried several positions. Not one to sit around, are you?"

"No, sir." She'd clasped her hands. "I...I took some time to get acclimated when I arrived but after a while I felt the need to do something."

He nodded. "Not unusual for the young ones. It's those who lived their full lifespan who are happy to relax."

She breathed a little easier at the news. She wasn't a complete oddity.

"You've tried being on the birthday party team."

"Yes, but I'm not very good at baking cakes and blowing up the balloons made me light-headed."

"I see." He turned another page. "Your stint in rainbow management wasn't successful either?"

"Not really. Apparently, I over-used them and it caused some confusion on the human plane."

"Upsetting what the human scientists believe can cause issues."

"So I was told." She winced at the memory.

"Your work in archives was quite commendable. It says here they are sorry to see you go." Michael arched a brow at her. "Why did you leave that position?"

"It was too similar to what I had done when I was alive. I...I want to do something where I can make a real difference, where I can help people. Something with a bit more potential for...adventure."

"Adventure? You're the daring kind?"

"I'd like to be. I mean, I think I was meant to be, but," she frowned. "My earthly life didn't provide much opportunity for it. You see, I take after my grandmother,

Suzette. She and I had some wonderful times together when I was a child but my parents never approved of her, saying she was too unconventional and they didn't want me to turn out like her. They ensured I knew the importance of following rules and…" Her voice trailed off as she realized she was rambling.

"I understand." Michael's smile was almost kindly for a moment before he began to study the final page of her application. "As you know, most GAs are extremely brave. Regular angels who apply for the position are required to cite examples from their human life that support their claim of suitability. Not many pass scrutiny. I see here you say you rescued a…teddy bear?" His brows shot upward. "Is that a typo?"

Any hope she might have had vanished at his expression. She'd never done anything even remotely brave in her entire life and all she'd been able to think of was her final act, trying to save the child's toy. In her desperation to get the job, she'd included the deed on her application. Too late, she realized how lame it was.

Her face grew warm under Michael's steady stare and she bit her lip, feeling tears beginning to prick. "I…I'm sorry. I…I shouldn't have—" She began to stand, assuming the interview had screeched to an end.

"Miss Winslow, stop." Michael interrupted her, setting down her application on his desk and resting his hands atop it. He opened his mouth to speak, closed it and seemed to consider his words before beginning again. "Miss Winslow…er…Eugenie, a guardian angel needs to be brave, daring. They need to think on their feet and react instantaneously to situations."

"I know." She hung her head and pressed her lips tightly together struggling to maintain her composure. For some reason, she'd pinned her hopes on this job, feeling drawn to it in a way she'd never experienced before.

Michael paused, then slowly exhaled. "Perhaps if you explained the circumstances surrounding your act of bravery...?"

"I..." A glance at him let her know this was her only chance—an exceedingly slim chance—to convince him to accept her on to his team. "Well, it all started when my parents left on a lecturing tour..." She related the events of her last two days of life and ended her tale with a comment about the child. "He looked so sad. All he wanted was his bear but his mother was in a hurry. I didn't stop to think, I just wanted to help him."

"Hmm..." Michael steepled his fingers and studied her through half-closed eyes, his lips slightly pursed. "As I said, a GA has to be daring and brave but more importantly, they need compassion. A warm and giving spirit."

Something in his tone encouraged her. Her heart began to beat faster and she held herself as still as possible, barely daring to move as she listened for his decision.

"You aren't exactly a textbook candidate but I sense potential
in you and am willing to take you under my wing, if you'll pardon the pun."

"Really?" She surged to her feet. "Oh, thank you. Thank you so much! I'll do whatever you ask. I'll work hard, I promise. You won't regret this."

"Eugenie," he'd leaned back and shook his head. "Lesson number one. No rambling. Please."

That had been last year. Since then she'd been studying, learning the ins and outs of being a guardian angel. She'd even had a few cases; aiding someone in finding their keys, assisting a child on their first day at a new school. And then that one heart-breaking case... She shook her head at the memory.

Of course, her cases were short and straight forward, only a few hours at most, never anything extended and complex like the senior GAs but she'd found some satisfaction in each assignment and her skills had slowly improved. Michael often commended her on following all three thousand eight hundred and twenty-two rules in the guardian angel handbook. She inwardly chuckled whenever he said that; if there was one thing her earthly life had prepared her for, it was dealing with rules!

Yes, she liked her new job better than anything she'd tried yet however, there was still a feeling of unrest within her. Was it more adventure she needed? More responsibility? Helping the man she'd found in the snow had left her feeling…excited? Fulfilled? Whatever the word, soon after the escapade, she'd hinted to Michael she'd like to try a bigger case. He'd responded with a considering look and the merest hint of a smile, then sent her off to continue to study the rule book. Having only been a GA for a short time, his response had been understandable, even if disappointing.

Now, barely a year later, she'd been surprised when a file had arrived for her early that morning along with a message to read the contents and appear before Michael at ten o'clock. The envelope itself had been unremarkable but when she'd viewed the file inside, her breathing had hitched.

It wasn't the ordinary green file she was used to or even yellow like she'd received for that one more urgent case. No, this one was red and the sight of it had caused her heart to begin hammering.

Some instinct, whether angelic senses or woman's intuition, was telling her it must mean something big, something different, maybe even a 'real' case!

She felt she was ready, having passed all the written tests that appeared at the end of each chapter of the rule book. Michael wouldn't have had her spend most of the last year learning the rules if they weren't important, right?

She'd carefully gone over the file Michael had sent. It contained details about a small town in Canada and she'd mentally patted herself on the back for having already explored that part of world. Yes, if this was going to be her big break, she was prepared and ready…she hoped.

A wave of doubt washed over her. She'd only been a GA for a little over a year. Was she really ready? After all, what did she really know beyond what was outlined in the rule book? Yet, surely the rule book must contain the most important bits of information, otherwise why did Michael put so much stock in it?

Ugh! What had she gotten herself into?

A glance at her watch had her jumping to her feet. It was almost time to meet with Michael and it wouldn't do to be late! She tucked the folder under her arm and hurried on her way.

Michael watched as his youngest GA entered his office and slid into the visitor's chair. She was breathing quickly, evidence she'd rushed to make sure she was on time. Eugenie was definitely a rule follower. It was one of the things he liked about her but, at the same time, it was one of the things that caused him to worry. She'd been raised in the early 1900s, a time when women had few rights and more often than not spent their lives as homemakers, bowing to the will of the male head of the household, following arbitrary rules. Such a life could easily stifle the spirit. At least hers hadn't been completely crushed; her snowy escapade last year had proven that. Of course, she didn't realize he was aware of everything his GAs did—that was a secret he kept tight to his chest—but it had certainly given him an indication of what she was capable of and where her future might lie.

She was settled in her chair now, her hands folded neatly in her lap just like always. The simple action made him smile.

"Good morning, Eugenie. How are you today?"

"I'm fine, sir." She furrowed her brow. "Well, to be honest, I'm actually a bit nervous. I was surprised to get a summons from you today and even though I've read over the file you sent, I'm not sure exactly why you wanted to see me." She stopped abruptly and pressed her lips together obviously realizing she was in danger of rambling.

He gave an approving nod at her attempt to curb the habit. "I asked you here today because I feel you're ready for a more challenging role as a GA. Your test scores have been excellent and the few assignments I've given you have been completed satisfactorily."

She bobbed her head. "Thank you, sir."

"No need for thanks. I give praise when praise is due." It was refreshing to have a respectful GA seated across from him. Some of the others were…well…. He mentally shook his head. Headstrong, rule-bending GAs were a subject for another time. Back to the matter at hand. "I have a case that needs a sensitive and delicate touch, something I believe you are able to deliver."

Eugenie's eyes widened and a smile appeared on her pretty face.

He'd known his announcement would please her. Would it continue to meet with her approval once she learned the details?

She clenched her hands and nodded. "Thank you, Michael. What do you need me to do?"

He leaned forward and nudged a manilla folder across the desk towards her.

She stared at it, eyes wide, making no move to reach for it.

Interesting. She claimed she wanted a greater challenge yet when presented with one, she hesitated. He hoped he wasn't pushing her too hard with this case.

"Look at the picture while I give you a rough outline." Relaxing back into his leather executive chair, he gave her a half-smile. "Your client's name is Benjamin Davis. Thirty-five. Divorced. No children."

She took the file and glanced at the photograph on the outside, looked back up at him and then her gaze suddenly snapped back to the photo, her eyes widening and her face paling. Michael noted her reaction but made no comment, continuing to share the details of the case.

"He recently lost his father after a lengthy illness. Dealing with his father's medical problems and then death, along with trying to keep his business solvent, has caused him to lose track of what was going on elsewhere in his life. The end result is that he has lost his faith. Faith in himself, in humankind, in the power of love and hope for the future."

"And it's my assignment to bring him back onto the path and into the light?"

Michael tapped a finger against his lips as he regarded the young angel in front of him. "Of a sort. There are many paths in life. Which path he ultimately takes is his choice. As to *faith*, there are many types of faith, not all of them religious in nature."

"But, how can I influence him? I've not had any experience interacting with clients yet. I've always been outside their cognizance."

"You are *not* to influence him, Eugenie. He is human and therefore has free will."

"But...?" She frowned, obviously confused.

"This case is a promotion of sort. You *will* be interacting with your client this time. He will be aware of your presence." He watched as her face paled and then grew rosy. Was she up to this? Her parents had kept her tethered to their ideals, a way of life that should have died with the Great War. She needed experience…experience of the world and of relationships. Something she never managed to achieve while alive but something this case could give her.

"I'm sorry, sir. I don't understand. I'm not allowed to influence him but I am encouraged to interact with him? Won't that, in itself, influence him?"

"Use your judgement, Eugenie. I trust you to do what is right."

Eugenie bit her lip trying to hide her shock as she once again stared at the photograph on the folder. It was him. Her unconscious man in the snow. With difficulty, she tried to stay composed while talking to her boss about the assignment. Fingering the edge of the file she wondered if she dared ask more questions. After a moment's hesitation, she decided to hold her tongue lest he think her incapable of handling the case.

"Thank you, Michael. I won't fail you or your trust in me." She stood up and, staring at the picture taped to the front of the folder in her hands, blindly left her superior's office.

Chapter 3

Ben Davis checked the measurement for the piece of wood he was about to cut. Measure twice, cut once; how often had his dad said those words to him? A hint of a smile curved his mouth as he remembered the man who had taught him the carpentry trade. The smile didn't last, of course. There wasn't much to smile about anymore. His dad was gone, buried almost twelve months.

The muscles in his jaw tightened at the memory. He'd done his best to make his father's last days comfortable, spending every minute he could spare with the man who had raised him single-handedly since the age of ten. But no amount of love or time had been able to stop the ravages of disease.

Ben flicked the switch on the saw, the roar of the power-tool an expression of his inner anger even if the sound did make him wince; the hangover he sported was rendering his head rather sensitive to the loud noise. Drinking himself into a stupor each night was stupid. He knew it, but it was the only way he could cope with the pile of fucked-up shit that was now his life.

While he'd been caring for his dying parent, his wife had been having an affair with his business partner. By the time his father was buried, he was divorced, his construction company was bankrupt and his so-called friend had doctored the books in such a way that there was no proof the bastard had been skimming money from the firm.

Angrily, he shoved the board along the guide, watching as the saw sliced through the wood. When the board was cut, he flicked off the switch and the whine of the spinning blade faded away. After hefting the board to his shoulder, he crossed the room and set it on the pair of sawhorses that supported a similar piece of wood. Together, the pieces would form a rustic table, part of the collection of furniture he was building in the hopes of turning a small profit.

It was nothing like the big business dreams he'd had years ago. At the time, he couldn't wait to leave this small farm with its rundown buildings. Now he was thankful to even have a roof over his head. Though how long even that would last, he wasn't sure.

A cold nose nudged his hand and he bent to ruffle the fur of his companion, a mongrel of a dog named Chip.

"Hey, buddy."

The old dog swished his tail in response and Ben spent a few minutes petting the animal before it wandered into the corner for a nap. Chip had been his father's and he'd inherited the dog along with the few acres of rocky, unfarmable land, an old barn and the small house where he now lived and worked.

It was a far cry from the high-end house he'd built for his wife, Sabrina, in an upscale neighbourhood. Of course, she'd taken it as part of the divorce settlement. Her lawyer had claimed she'd been an aspiring model with the potential to earn millions yet she'd given it all up to help her husband expand his business. The house and its contents were compensation for those lost wages.

Yeah, right.

Not that he cared. The place had never felt like a home to him. He'd slept there and that was about it. Hell, towards the end of his father's life, he'd not even done that, spending the nights at the hospice not knowing his wife was screwing another man in his bed.

He scowled and grabbed a drill to make a pilot hole in the wood. Just as he set the drill bit to the wood and started the tool, someone unexpectedly spoke behind him.

"Hello."

"What the—?" In surprise, his hand jerked and the drill bit caught the edge of his finger, ripping off a generous chunk of skin. Blood began to drip everywhere and he swore loudly.

"Oh no! I'm so sorry! I didn't mean to startle you." A young woman stood beside him, her eyes wide as she stared at his injured hand for a moment before beginning to dig frantically in her purse. "This is all my fault. Let me help you. I know I have a bandage in here somewhere."

Ben pulled a rag out of his pocket and wrapped it around his hand. "No need to fuss. I'll see to it in a bit. What can I help you with?"

She pushed the door of the shop closed and shivered. "It's cold out there."

"Not that bad yet." He glanced out the window at the grey, overcast sky and shrugged. "It's only November. It'll get a lot worse once winter hits."

"I'm from England originally so this *is* cold for me." She gave him an apologetic smile and began to gravitate towards the old pot-bellied stove he used to keep the place warm, her gaze drifting around the interior of the building.

"Are you lost or...?"

"Oh, sorry. I...I saw the sign on the road about hand-crafted furniture for sale."

A potential customer. Maybe the day wasn't going to be a complete waste after all. "Okay. Well, look around while I go tend to this." He held up his rag-wrapped hand. "I'll be back in a minute to answer any questions you might have." As an afterthought he added a warning, "Don't touch any of the tools."

He gave a quick glance at Chip, thinking he should tell her not to worry about the dog but the animal was still curled up in its bed, fast asleep. Some guard dog!

Through the dirty, cobwebbed window Eugenie watched the man, Benjamin, leave the warmth of the barn and walk over to the house. On the few cases she'd been assigned, most of her time had been spent invisible, drifting along beside her clients unbeknownst to them, doling out bits of help as needed but never interacting with them. Now, she was in unfamiliar territory. What should she do next? Follow him right into his house? Waiting in this outbuilding while her assignment went off on his own didn't seem right. What if he needed help with that cut? There *had* been an awful lot of blood. Having already saved his life once she now felt responsible for him. Deciding to go with her gut, she left the relative comfort of the barn.

She headed towards the house only to pause when she realized the dog was following her. When she'd noticed it sleeping in the corner, she'd wondered how it would greet her. Would it remember her or not? Apparently, it did, for it sniffed at her feet, looked up at her and wagged its tail in greeting.

"Hello again, dog." She'd forgotten how large the animal was. Its feet were enormous and its head came up to her waist. Thankfully she had proof of its benign nature. After all, hadn't it snuggled to her side last year, sharing its body warmth? Her parents had always declared dogs to be filthy, dangerous beasts, however, based on her experience with this one, she believed they had overstated the case.

The big golden-brown dog sat down beside her and cocked its head as if questioning her motives.

"I'm here to help your owner, okay? Just like last time."

The animal huffed a muffled woof, stood and padded its way towards the house.

Taking that as permission, she followed and climbed the old wooden steps at the back of the house, then eased open the door. The dog brushed past her and headed towards a water bowl where it began to drink noisily.

"You want me to just make myself at home, right?"

Of course, the dog didn't answer, so she began to look about. She was in a small, narrow, utility room with a washing machine, sink and shelves along one wall. The other held hooks for coats and a place for boots. Beyond that there was a door frame with a missing door and what looked like a kitchen just beyond. Leaving the dog to his own devices, she began to explore further.

Her first impression was horror. Never had she seen such a messy kitchen. It didn't look like the room had been cleaned in months.

The counters were covered in empty cans and packages. Dishes were piled in a sink filled with water, bits of congealed grease clinging to the edges and mold showing on the surfaces that weren't submerged. Just the thought of the number of germs hiding in among the trash and unwashed crockery made her shudder and look away.

A photo on the fridge caught her attention. It appeared to be Benjamin standing with someone, except the image was partially covered by a magnet. She stepped closer for a better look. Yes, it was her client, but with whom?

Moving the magnet aside, she idly noted it was shaped like a dog-bone and bore the number of a pet store on it. Interestingly enough, there seemed to be actual tooth marks gouged into the plastic as well. She gave the dog a suspicious look, then returned her attention to the photograph. It depicted a laughing and relaxed Benjamin Davis with a pretty, statuesque, blonde woman tucked to his side.

She frowned, thinking of her own lack of inches and plain brown hair, only to be jerked from her thoughts by something cold and wet nudging her. It was the dog nuzzling the biscuit shaped magnet in her hand.

"Sorry, but this is a magnet not a real dog biscuit. You've tried to eat it before. See the tooth marks?"

Apparently, the dog didn't believe her for it snuffled at the magnet again, his whiskers tickling her hand. She stifled a giggle and was about to put the picture and magnet back in place when she heard footsteps in the hallway. She fumbled the magnet and it dropped to the floor.

The dog gave a happy woof and dived for the plastic bone causing it to skitter across the floor.

"No! Don't eat it. Bad dog!" She ducked under the table and wrested the magnet from the animal who gave her a woeful look and then lumbered back towards the door.

The magnet was now slimy with dog slobber and bits of dust. Making a face, she picked it up gingerly and began to crawl out from under the table. She was still on her hands and knees when Benjamin entered the room.

"What do you think you're doing?"

There was no mistaking the accusation in his voice and Eugenie swallowed hard as she peeked up at him from her position on the floor.

"I...er...I thought you might need help with the bandages."

He folded his arms. "And you believed I kept them under the kitchen table?"

She felt her face grow warm. "No, of course not." Struggling to her feet, she banged her head on the table edge. "Ouch!" She staggered to the side a bit and Benjamin grabbed her arm to steady her.

"You okay?"

"Yes, more surprised than hurt." She rubbed her head with her free arm all the while extremely aware of the heat of his body so close to hers, the manly smell of sawdust and sweat filling her lungs as she inhaled.

He gave an indecipherable grunt and released his hold on her noticing the magnet she still held in her hand. Immediately, his gaze flew to the fridge and his brows lowered into a scowl.

"Couldn't resist snooping, could you? Women! You're all alike."

"No, I wasn't—"

"Did Sabrina send you? Did she run through all the money she bled from me already? Well, you can damn well tell her there's nothing left. Look around." He swept his arm out in an encompassing manner. "An old table, a stove with only two working burners.   If she wants it, she can have it for all its worth."

Eugenie shook her head. "No. I don't know who Sabrina is. I came in to see if you needed help. Really. And then I saw the picture on the fridge and...and..." She stuttered to a halt. "I'm sorry." How many times had she apologized to him already? This assignment was *not* off to a good start.

Benjamin shook his head and pinched the bridge of his nose. "I'm sorry, too. I shouldn't have yelled at you."

Spying the photograph on the floor, she bent and picked it up. "Here."

He looked at the picture she held out and then took it.

"And the magnet. It's sort of sticky. Your dog was chewing on it." She handed over the bit of plastic as well.

He wiped it on his shirt and stuck it back up on the fridge.

Eugenie flicked a glance at the picture again. "Is that her? Sabrina?"

"Yeah. My ex." His jaw tightened.

"I'm sorry." Oh, good heavens, she'd just said it again. He was going to think she didn't know how to say anything else.

"No need. I'm better off without her."

"Then why do you keep her picture on the fridge?" She cocked her head, trying to understand.

"To remind me not to be fooled by a pretty face again."

"Oh." She shifted on her feet, not sure what to say next.

Ben took a deep breath and blew it out. "You said you were here to see the furniture?"

Recognizing the conversation was over, she nodded and then followed him out to the barn. Once there, she spent some time looking at the various pieces. They truly were lovely.

"If you're interested, I only accept cash." He shoved his hands in his pockets.

"I'm definitely interested." She ran her hand over the back of a chair. "Do you deliver?"

"I can if it's in town. Out of town, I'll have to add extra to the price to cover the cost of gas."

"Okay." She gave him a smile. "I'll be back tomorrow to pick out a few things."

He nodded but his eyes had narrowed into a wary look. "Sure."

It was obvious he didn't believe her. Michael was right. Benjamin Davis certainly lacked faith in his fellow man…er…woman. Well, she'd do her best to fix that. As his guardian angel, it was her duty!

With a final nod of thanks, she left the shop, her mind already busy on all she needed to do. The first thing was obvious. She'd need to find a place to stay in town if she was going to have him deliver furniture tomorrow!

Ben watched the woman walk to the road. Yeah, she wouldn't be back. Women never meant what they said. She was a pretty little thing though. And something about her was vaguely familiar, though he couldn't place from where.

He shook his head and was about to return to the job he'd been working on earlier when a sound near the road drew his attention. Through narrowed eyes he watched as the mailman placed something in his mailbox and then drove away. Most likely more bills.

His shoulders slumped as he walked to the mailbox and opened the old metal container. Yep it was filled with bills; electricity, natural gas, credit cards, the lumber yard, the bank. Was there anyone in the world he didn't owe money to?

He ran his hand through his hair and looked around. All he had left was his tools and the clothes on his back. The old pickup truck he'd bought still had money owing on it. The farm was mortgaged. Everything in the house was old, the appliances on their last legs. How had it all come to this?

"I'm sorry, Dad." He glanced skyward. His father had loved this place but if things didn't turn around soon the bank would take possession of it. "You always told me a man paid his debts, he didn't walk away from his responsibilities, but I don't know what other options are left."

Stuffing the envelopes into his pocket, he headed back to the barn. Working with wood always soothed him and helped him think. The table would be a nice piece when it was done especially if he carved some extra detailing into the legs.

He reached for the drill he'd been using earlier and promptly banged his injured finger. Ah hell! Blood began to seep from under the bandage again.

Cursing he stomped back to the house. Why had he even bothered getting out of bed today?

Eugenie was already back in the locker room in Heaven before she realized she hadn't given Benjamin her name. Well, too late now. She could do that tomorrow when she had an actual address. But how did she go about getting one? She'd never lived anywhere on Earth other than with her parents. How did you find a place and, once you found one, how did you pay for it? She would die of embarrassment if she had to ask Michael all those questions.

"Afternoon, Eugenie." The sound of a male voice had her turning and she noticed another GA, Zeke, entering the locker room. She'd shared several conversations with him over the past few months and he'd been very welcoming when she'd joined the squadron, helping her with her locker that first day when it had refused to open. His ready smile had eased her nerves even though his formal robes had made him seem intimidating.

Since then, they'd developed an easy camaraderie which meant she didn't hesitate to ask his help on this, her first big case.

"Zeke! You're just the person I need."

"Really? You need me? Eugenie, I didn't know you cared." He pressed a hand to his heart and gave her a goofy grin that had her laughing.

"How droll, Zeke."

"*Droll?* Really, Eugenie?"

She pursed her lips and shook her head. "It's a perfectly good word! Now, please try to be serious for just a few minutes. I have a new assignment and for the first time I need to have a physical presence on Earth."

"An interactive case? Congrats! You're moving up the ranks fast." He leaned against a locker and gave her a nod of approval.

"Thank you. I'm quite excited about it. The only problem is I don't know how to do it."

"Now, that's not true. I know you know how to materialize."

"Yes, I can do that. It's all the small details like renting an apartment and obtaining money that has me worried."

"Didn't you do the seminar on All Things Human?"

"No. Not yet. Michael's had me studying the rule book and taking the chapter tests."

"That's strange. Michael's usually on top of things. If you were scheduled for interaction assignments, he should have had you enrolled in classes." Zeke frowned then gave a shrug. "I guess this case must have come up unexpectedly and he feels you have the needed skills for it."

"I suppose, but right now I feel decidedly *unskilled.* Help?"

Zeke pushed off from the locker. His chest seemed to swell, his shoulders straightening. "Babe, you've come to the right man. I know all there is to know about living on earth. My former partner, Alex, kept a pad down there and lived as a human. First off, you need to go to Acquisitions. They'll furnish you with enough fake documentation to carry you through the assignment."

"Fake?"

"Yeah, we don't perma-change the records on earth for an assignment unless absolutely necessary but don't worry, these are good enough to pass inspection."

"Slow down! I need to take notes!"

Zeke chuckled and led her to a bench. "Let's sit down. This could take a while."

Eugenie took out a pen and a pad of paper and began to scribble notes while Zeke continued to talk.

"After you have your documentation, you need to go to the bursar's office and get a 450 form. Fill it out and you'll get a cash advance and a credit card. They'll also set up a bank account for you and explain how to use it and a debit card. Ask for Pete, tell him you're a friend of mine and he'll see you right."

"Ask for Pete..." She murmured the words as she finished writing them down.

"Good. Now, while you're doing that I'll ask permission to help you on the human plane. I'm already helping on another case but I'm sure Michael won't mind if I split my time between the two." He rubbed his hands together and appeared to be thinking. "We need to get you some clothes—"

"What's wrong with what I'm wearing?"

Zeke looked her up and down and shook his head. "Look at the dress you're wearing. Way too retro."

"But your formal robes are even more so and you wear them all the time," she pointed out.

"Oh…er…but not on a real case. This," he plucked at his white gown, "is my signature style."

"Signature style?" She raised her brows.

"No?" He looked surprised and rubbed his chin. "Maybe I need to reconsider…"

"About my case?" She drew his attention back to her problem.

"Oh, right." He gave her a critical look. "You're going to need jeans and t-shirts, yoga pants, casual shoes, the whole works if you're going to fit in on earth. At least you've taken advantage of the amenities up here and had your hair cut at some point during the last century, so we can skip that step."

"Okay," she nodded, thankful at least something about her appearance was satisfactory.

"I'll help you find somewhere to live. You gotta be careful down there. People would question why a young woman is wandering around by herself. Little things like that can blow your cover.

"Blowing my cover." Her stomach gave a little flop at the very idea. "That's one of the things I'm worried about."

"You'll be fine." Zeke gave her a shoulder bump. "A lot of it is instinct. The main thing to remember is to not be seen using your powers."

"Powers?" She stared at him blankly. "I don't have any yet beyond flying and all the angels can do that."

"Are you kidding me? You have a whole range of powers…or you should." Zeke's forehead wrinkled in a frown.

Eugenie shook her head. "I know some GAs can do amazing things but I'm still a beginner, remember?"

"Oh boy!" Zeke shook his head slightly. "Sorry, Babe, I keep forgetting you weren't born to the position like moi, so your GA powers need to be learned as they're not part of your genetic make-up. But don't worry, the longer you're up here, the stronger your powers get.

"Think of it like a video or computer game. As you advance – or in this case the longer you live up here as a GA – you get extra health and strength. Even the short time you've been a GA should have been enough to give you a few extra abilities. You probably just haven't discovered them yet. And Michael should've given you a power boost when you got this assignment. He gave me one when I got my first big job."

"Power boost? No, I don't think he did." She frowned, totally confused.

"Huh. Well, perhaps Michael thought you were ready. I'm damned sure I wasn't ready when I got my first real case." He shrugged. "But as I said, it's like this video game. You—"

She had to interrupt him. "Zeke, I don't *play* video games. For that matter, I've no idea how to even use a computer."

"You don't? What do you do in your down time?"

"Er… I read."

Zeke's look of incredulousness was a work of art. "Oh, Eugenie, honey, you have so much to learn. I tell you what, while we're looking for a place for you to crash I'd better give you a quick run-through on GA 101 and life in the 21st Century."

The following afternoon Eugenie was riding the bus back to Benjamin Davis' home. It had been an interesting twenty-four hours. Zeke might still be considered a young GA but he knew so much that she didn't. She was currently the proud possessor of a rental contract on a small apartment in an old house. Just two rooms with bath and a kitchenette but it was all she needed. It was only temporary after all.

Her wallet now had cash in it and a plastic rectangular thing called a credit card and another that was apparently a debit card, different from a credit card and she was still somewhat confused over the difference. Zeke had shown her how to use it because she hadn't been able to make head nor tail of Pete's explanation. Her fellow GA had also called into question her command of the English language. Apparently, her vocabulary was singularly old-fashioned.

And... she'd just missed her bus stop!

With a sigh, she waited and exited the bus a couple of blocks further on than she wanted.

"Pay attention next time," she chided herself.

Retracing her route, she couldn't help but notice how clean the streets looked, how fresh the air smelled. Back when she was alive, winter was more likely to be foggy, the air choked with fumes from a myriad of coal fires. The air here was invigorating and trees dotted the landscape rather than rows of buildings. Even though the branches were now devoid of leaves they still looked picturesque against the clear blue sky.

Benjamin's house was at the end of a long road some distance from the main thoroughfare and not really on the bus route at all. Her intended stop was as close as she could get and now she had at least another mile to walk. The paved road became a gravel road and then more of a dirt pathway with ruts from the car tires. She placed her feet carefully, not wanting to turn her ankle. As an angel, she'd recover quickly, it would still hurt like the blazes in the meantime.

She slowed as Benjamin's home came into view. Despite having seen it before, this was the first time she was really taking in its rundown appearance. In its day, the building must have been a cute little place but now the shutters were crooked and the paint was peeling. Dead weeds filled the flower beds and the fence was partially falling down. The entire place gave an air of being tired. Similar to its owner, she thought.

The dog came loping out to greet her as she walked down the driveway. It greeted her as if she were an old friend.

"Hello, dog." She scratched his ears and then followed him as he led the way back to the barn where Benjamin would be working. The building was in no better condition than the rest of the place. The red paint was faded and the windows were covered with cobwebs and a thick layer of dust. Even the door seemed rickety, hardly suitable to keep out the weather or intruders.

Oddly enough, there was no sound of hammering or sawing coming from the building. Had he injured himself again? Her heart began to pound at the idea of him lying on the ground bleeding and she yanked open the door and rushed in. Immediately, the smell of stale alcohol hit her, drowning out the aroma of new wood and sawdust.

The room was dimly lit and she fumbled for a switch, flicking the lights on, wondering what was going on. The return of brightness was accompanied by a string of curses. Following the sound, she found Benjamin sitting on an old wooden crate, his elbows on his knees, cradling his head in his hands. The nearby stove was stone-cold and she wondered why he hadn't lit it yet.

"Benjamin?"

He looked up at her with bloodshot eyes, his face sporting a day's worth of whiskers. "Don't yell." He winced as if even the sound of his own voice were too loud.

"I'm not yelling, I—" She took a step closer and then cocked her head, reassessing the situation. He was hungover!

"Benjamin Davis! What have you been up to?" She planted her hands on her hips and used the sternest tone she could muster.

He frowned at her. "I know you. You're that girl..." He waved his hand as if trying to marshal his thoughts.

"Yes, I'm the girl that was here yesterday. I said I'd be back."

"Didn't think you meant it." He gave a heavy sigh and pushed himself upright.

"That doesn't explain why you're totally cropsick this morning! You must have been absolutely blotto last night to be in such a condition at this hour of the day."

"Cropsick? Blotto?" He shook his head then let out a groan as if the action had pained him. "What are you talking about?"

"Hungover and drunk." She winced. Zeke was right. She obviously needed to update her language skills.

"Well, I was drinking because I wanted to, not that it's any of your business."

She pressed her lips together. "I suppose it isn't. However, you *do* run a business and I'm here as a customer and I expect some service. Now, light the stove. It's freezing in here." She rubbed her hands up and down her arms.

"All right, all right. No need to nag." He crouched down and set to work on the stove.

The dog appeared at her side, a scrunched-up piece of paper in its mouth. She took it and smoothed it out. It appeared to be a bill of some sort. A demand for payment from a bank. From the looks of it, Benjamin was in serious debt. Her buying one or two pieces of furniture wouldn't dig him out of the hole he'd found himself in.

"Hey, where did you get that?" Benjamin snatched the paper from her hand.

"Your dog gave it to me."

"Chip?" He glanced at the dog who was now settling in beside the stove for a nap.

"Is that his name? Very appropriate given you're a carpenter."

"My dad named him. Chip was his dog and I inherited him along with the rest of this place."

"Inherited? Your father passed away?" She reached out and touched his arm. "I'm so sorry for your loss."

"Yeah, well, he's in a better place now, or so they say." A muscle ticked in his jaw.

"He is indeed. Never doubt that." She rushed to reassure him and then stopped not wanting to give herself away. A change of topic was in order and fast. "I notice you seem to owe a lot of money."

"Not your concern." He shoved the bill in his pocket. "So, you came back to buy something?"

"Yes, I'll take your entire inventory."

He rolled his eyes. "Don't be ridiculous. You probably live in a small apartment and barely have room for a decent-sized table." Arms folded, he fixed her with a cold look. "And besides that, I'm not some damned charity case."

"I guess my statement was a bit impulsive. My place *is* too small to hold all this but I really do wish I could purchase more." She held up her hand to stop him when he opened his mouth to speak. "Not as an act of charity but because the furniture really is lovely."

He studied her for a moment before nodding. "Thanks."

"However, maybe I do know some people who might be interested in buying a few pieces." She thought of

Zeke's former partner who lived on earth; maybe he'd purchase something. And hadn't her new landlord mentioned redecorating?

"Why are you trying to help? You have some kind of guardian angel complex or something?"

She felt the blood drain from her face. He couldn't know, could he? A nervous laugh escaped her. "Of course not. It's like I said. I know a few people."

"And I'm a billionaire disguised as a washed-up carpenter."

"You're not washed-up, Benjamin!"

"Then what do you call this?" He flicked a glance around the workshop before frowning. "And how do you know my name?"

"I...I heard it in town when I was asking where to buy furniture." She surreptitiously crossed her fingers behind her back hoping he wouldn't ask where. Thankfully, he didn't.

"Yeah, well, call me Ben. Benjamin is what my ex called me." He rubbed the back of his neck. "What do you want to buy?"

Chapter 4

Ben glanced out of the corner of his eye as he steered his old truck down the road. The woman who sat beside him was a bit of a mystery. She seemed to have appeared out of nowhere and yet he couldn't shake the feeling he knew her. It niggled at the back of his mind, just out of reach.

She was a pretty little thing. Light brown hair that skimmed her shoulders, hazel eyes that revealed her emotions. And she seemed to have a good heart, wanting to help even though she was a bit too nosey in his opinion.

He returned his gaze to the road and frowned. The table and chairs she'd bought would give him a bit of cash. Not enough to pay off his debt to the lumberyard but at least he'd be able to put gas in the truck. He sure hoped she'd been telling the truth when she said she knew people who wanted to buy his furniture. His luck had been going steadily downhill for the past year and he'd pretty much hit rock bottom. If things didn't turn around soon, he didn't know what he'd do.

"We turn here." The girl pointed to the left and he slowed the vehicle.

"What's your name?" It suddenly struck him he didn't know anything about her.

"Eugenie Suzette Winslow." She kept her eyes trained out the window, a smile curving her lips as if she was truly loving the passing scenery.

"That's quite a mouthful."

"Yes." She sighed. "My father was a professor of ancient languages but he loved European poetry and literature. I'm named for a French writer who lived early in the eighteen hundreds and for my grandmother."

He nodded and silence fell between them until she indicated the place where she lived.

"I have an apartment upstairs here."

"This is quite an old building." He eyed the rambling Victorian as he climbed out of the truck and rounded to the back where he flipped the tailgate down.

"Yes, but the rent was affordable."

He made a non-committal sound and hefted the table in his arms then turned to Eugenie. "Lead the way."

The exterior staircase was steep and he had some doubts about what kind of place she might be living in. Some old houses that were subdivided into apartments could be in pretty rough shape and he'd hate to think of her living in a dive. Once they reached her actual apartment, it seemed to be a nice enough place, though sparsely furnished. She could definitely use the furniture she'd bought.

"Where do you want this?"

"Over by the window. I can sit and enjoy the view."

He set the table down and helped her arrange it in place, their hands brushing. It was a brief contact but enough to have him pausing and looking up at her. Her eyes were focused on where they'd touched and then she slowly lifted her gaze to his face. A flush stained her cheeks before she jerked her hand back.

"I..uh...think this is the right place for the table."

He nodded. "I'll get the chairs." As he made his way downstairs, he told himself he had *not* had a reaction to her. He'd sworn off women. He didn't need another complication in his life. But...damn, it was cute how she got flustered so easily!

A short time after Ben had left, there was a thudding sound on Eugenie's door as if someone were kicking it, followed by the sound of Zeke's voice, "Hey, Eugenie. I've got something for you."

"What are you doing out there? Can't you knock like a normal person?" She yanked the door open then stared. "Oh."

Zeke was standing with a large box in his hands. A television. She'd seen them in Heaven but had never been interested in watching any of the entertainment broadcast on them.

"Your landlord said this place was cable ready, so all we need to do is plug this baby in."

"Zeke, I don't need a television."

"Sure you do. It's a perfect way to stay current with cultural changes." He set the box down and unpacked the device. "And it will help you upgrade your language skills."

"Hmm... I hadn't thought of that."

Zeke grinned at her and tapped his head. "This brain of mine did. Stick with me, kid, and I'll have you up to speed in no time!" He plugged in the TV and began to give her a crash course in using a remote control.

The next morning Eugenie stood in front of the appliance called a microwave. Her landlord had pointed it out to her when he'd given her a quick tour of the place, mentioning it was brand new. Experimentally, she poked at a few of the buttons but nothing happened. The washer and dryer had proven similarly mysterious and had left her feeling ill-equipped to manage on her own. It would seem modern living wasn't as easy as people said it was. When she'd lived with her parents, they'd had hired help to cook and clean.

Turning from the mysterious devices, she decided it would be more prudent to spend her time speaking to someone about Ben's furniture. She'd have a word with Brent, her landlord, and then go find Zeke.

It turned out Brent was quite receptive to the idea of buying from a local craftsman. He'd just finished renovating the main floor of the building which he occupied and was now in the redecorating stage.

"Yeah, I need a new bedroom set for this room." Brent had looked down at her from the ladder where he was perched, carefully painting the decorative moldings that framed the ceiling.

"I'm sure you'll find something you like. Ben does amazing work." She'd watched as Brent applied a final swipe of paint and then climbed down to wipe his hands on a rag.

"I'll stop by tomorrow and take a look around." He'd hefted the ladder on his shoulder and moved to the other side of the room.

Eugenie left him to his painting and headed back to Heaven feeling she was making good progress. Zeke was next on her list for finding potential buyers for Ben's furniture. When she finally tracked the GA down, he was in the arcade playing some game called Space Invaders according to the name on the machine.

"Hi, Eugenie." He barely flicked a look at her, his attention focused on the screen in front of him. "I know this is almost archaic but I love the old games. How's the apartment working out?"

"It's lovely but there are so many appliances that I have absolutely no idea how to use."

"Don't worry about it, Babe. Next time I'm there it'll take me two minutes to show you how to operate them.

"But what if someone is in the apartment with me and they spill wine on their shirt and I need to wash it?"

"Just soak it in the sink."

She sighed and decided fine details like that might not be Zeke's forte. "Anyway, that's not what I need to ask you about."

Zeke didn't take his eyes off the screen while he pressed buttons to shoot down electronic aliens. "How can I help?"

"My client needs to sell the furniture he's made to get out of debt. Once he's solvent again I'm sure he'll be able to make a success of his life; he's very talented." She paused, the thought of her client causing her to smile. "I was wondering… You mentioned you had a partner who preferred to live on the human plane. Do you think he might need any furniture?"

"Furniture? It's possible. And I'll ask around." Zeke became focused on his game again and Eugenie decided to leave him to it in the hope that he would remember to ask his friend without her needing to remind him.

She left the arcade and headed towards Michael's office to report what she'd done. According to the rule book, she didn't need to check in every day. However, this was her first assignment that required actually making contact and she wanted to confirm she was on the right track. She tugged open the heavy plate glass door that formed the entrance of the building while mentally rehearsing what she'd say to her boss.

"Eugenie."

The sound of Michael's voice intruded on her thoughts and she looked up to see the archangel standing in front of her.

"Hello, sir. I was just coming to see you."

"Is there a problem?" Michael's brows rose but he gestured with his hand for her to follow him as they made their way across the lobby.

"Well, my client seems to be experiencing severe financial difficulties so I'm trying to arrange the sale of some of his hand-crafted furniture." She cocked her head. "I don't suppose you need a new table or chair?

He shook his head, his lips seeming to twitch as he pushed the elevator button. "Not at the moment."

"Oh." She frowned and then followed him inside as the doors to the elevator slid open. "I'm sure if he was financially secure, it would solve all his problems."

Michael nodded slowly. "Financial security is important; however, money doesn't buy happiness, Eugenie."

"I know, but—"

"Benjamin Davis has several personal demons he still needs to tackle."

"I'm not sure what you mean?"

"Think about it, Eugenie. How well do you really know the man?" Michael exited the elevator and she trotted along beside him.

"Well," She frowned. "I know he's in debt, his father passed away and his house is a mess."

"Surface facts. Spend some time with him. Learn what actually makes him tick. Get to know the man inside the gruff exterior. A GA has to come to an in-depth understanding of his or her client before they can truly know when an assignment is complete."

Her shoulders slumped. "I guess there's a lot more to this than I realized."

"I suggest you head back to the human plane and try to find a way to become part of Mr. Davis' life." Michael stopped walking, having reached the door to his office.

"Any suggestions?"

Michael gave her a pat on the shoulder. "You're a clever girl. I'm sure you'll come up with something."

Eugenie watched Michael disappear into his office and pursed her lips. Become part of Ben's life. But how? Continuously buying more furniture would make him suspicious. She supposed she could tell him she'd asked her friends if they, or anyone they knew, would like to buy some of his pieces. But that conversation wouldn't qualify as a prolonged interaction.

No, she needed to be in his life for an extended period of time, if she'd understood Michael correctly. She thought of Ben's house, of the mess it was in. Offer to be his housekeeper? That wouldn't work either; he couldn't afford one of those. And it would be a daunting job. From what she'd seen of his house and the workshop, both spaces were jam-packed with things. The entire property needed a thorough organizing starting with clearing out all the old objects she'd noticed stacked in the corners.

An idea began to formulate. One of the TV shows she'd watched the previous night had been about people finding old collectibles. Perhaps she could claim she was a buyer for an antique store and ask if she could sort through Ben's place under the premise that old stuff was like hidden treasure. If she understood the show correctly, everyday things from decades ago could be worth money if the right buyer was found. Ben could certainly use some extra cash and getting his surroundings sorted out would be bound to help him feel better. How anyone could live with all that clutter was beyond her!

Ben rubbed his chin, puzzled yet pleased at the sale he'd just made. After several weeks of no one even setting foot on his property, he'd finally had a customer. He'd not really believed Eugenie, but it appeared she'd followed through; her landlord had stopped by and purchased an entire bedroom set including a headboard, armoire, night tables and chest of drawers. He'd thought at best he'd sell one piece. This was...well...it was like a miracle, except he didn't believe in those.

Miracles didn't happen to guys like him. He'd come to that conclusion as a child when his mother had died and no amount of praying had brought her back. And then, he'd thought his ex was his personal angel only she turned out to be a money-hungry user. And he couldn't forget what had happened to his father. He'd broken down and prayed for his father to be cured, but as usual it had been a waste of time. That had confirmed the fact in his mind that there was no one to rely on in this life except yourself.

Well, maybe he could rely on Eugenie...a bit. He watched the van drive away with nearly a thousand dollars' worth of furniture. Eugenie had been as good as her word. Too bad it wouldn't last. One day of good sales would help, but it was a drop in the ocean to what he still needed to pull his ass out of the fire.

He bent down and scratched Chip's ears. "At least I can buy you another bag of dog food and a few groceries for myself. Make a payment to the bank as well." He'd had to remortgage the farm to help pay off the pile of debts his erstwhile partner had left and now he was falling behind in the repayment.

He straightened and turned to walk to the house only to bump into Eugenie.

"Hey!"

"Hello, Ben." She smiled up at him.

"Where did you come from?"

"Didn't you see me walking down the road?"

"No."

"Maybe you were too busy helping to load furniture onto that van."

"Yeah," he frowned. "That must have been it." He was sure he would have noticed her approaching or that Chip would have at least barked. Odd.

"I see my landlord was here." Eugenie peered around him and then stepped inside the barn.

"Yeah, he's a nice guy. Knew exactly what he was looking for." Ben followed her. The place was a lot emptier than it had been yesterday.

"I was sure he would come by." Hands clasped behind her back, Eugenie wandered to the rear of the building. "I see you have a lot of old stuff stored back here."

He nodded. "This place belonged to my grandfather and then my dad. Neither of them ever threw anything out. Over the years, quite a collection of junk has piled up. I need to clear it out someday. Rent a dumpster and start pitching things into it."

"No!" Eugenie turned to him, aghast. "You can't do that. This so-called *junk* could be worth a small fortune."

He looked at the pile of rusted and worn objects. "Nah. There's nothing important in there."

"I beg to differ. I'm somewhat of an expert on the early twentieth century and I can assure you there is a market for your father's things."

"Really?" He scratched his head.

She nodded. "I'd like to make you a business proposal. Let me sort through and sell these items. I'm sure you'll be pleasantly surprised by how much money we can get for them."

"What's in it for you? What's your angle?" He braced himself. Here it comes, he thought to himself. This is where she tries to rip him off.

"Angle?"

"Yeah. Nobody does work for free. How much do you want?"

She hesitated. He could see her thoughts racing and he braced himself for an exorbitant fee.

"Would ten percent be too much?"

"Ten?" He frowned. It wasn't what he'd been expecting. So instead of trying to scam him, she was treating him like a charity case. His lips tightened. He might be up against it, but he still had some pride. "I told you I'm not looking for a handout."

"Well, then make it fifteen but no more." She held up her hand even as he opened his mouth to protest. "I'll get a great deal of personal satisfaction going through these items. I have a passion for old things." She turned and scanned the items and when she spoke again there was a definite sincerity to her tone. "Please, let me do this. I'll really enjoy myself."

He narrowed his eyes, considering her proposal. It would be good to get the place cleaned up. It had always driven him slightly crazy to see the clutter with which his father had surrounded himself. And if Eugenie did the sorting and selling, he'd have time to continue with his woodwork. Given the sales today, he had to restock the shop. He looked at her again. There was almost a glow about her as she contemplated the pile of junk. Go figure!

Eventually he gave a nod. "Okay. It's a deal."

"Great!" Eugenie beamed at him and stuck out her hand to shake on the arrangement.

As their palms touched that feeling of awareness filled him once again, shooting up his arm to his heart, warming him in a way he hadn't felt in years.

An odd expression passed over Eugenie's face and he had a feeling she was experiencing the same thing. That would never do. Quickly, he let go of her hand and stepped back. This was going to be a business arrangement and nothing else.

Nothing. Else. At. All.

Chapter 5

Eugenie spent the following morning talking to her neighbours, trying to convince them they needed to visit Ben's shop and buy some of his furniture. Unfortunately, the only success she'd had was with Brent. He was extremely pleased with his purchases from the previous day and had already been planning on buying one more chair. She frowned as she remembered her landlord's final remarks.

"Eugenie, that man is not only talented, he's also downright gorgeous. Too bad he doesn't bat for my team."

The conversation still puzzled her. Bat for what team? As far as she knew cricket wasn't played in the winter. Or maybe it was baseball, since they were in North America. She'd have to ask Zeke about that particular phrase.

As she walked down the road to Ben's place, she hoped Zeke had managed to convince his ex-partner to buy something. While she was trying to sound positive about earning money from the sale of the items piled at the back of the building, she wasn't sure how much they would actually make. If it were possible, she'd hire herself out and give the money to Ben but she doubted he'd accept it plus she had no marketable skills. According to the TV shows she'd been watching, modern women held down a wide variety of jobs outside the home. The very concept was quite foreign to her and she suspected she'd have great difficulty fitting in to modern life. No, if she was going to help Ben, it had to be here on the farm where her old-fashioned ways wouldn't stand out so much.

The door to the barn was ajar and she entered to find Ben hard at work.

"Hello, Ben!"

"Hi!" He looked up at her from where he was crouched down fitting two pieces of wood together. "I was wondering if you'd be back today or if you'd changed your mind."

"Oh, don't worry, I'm not about to do that." She wondered if it was just her imagination that his expression seemed to brighten at her words. And she noted there was no hint of alcohol in the air. Good. Her gaze drifted to the chair he was working on. "That's nice."

"Thanks. Your landlord called this morning and said he wanted it. I guess there was an empty corner in the room or something. Anyway, it means I can't help you with the sorting until I get this finished."

"That's okay. If I need any help, I'll give a shout."

He gave a nod and they both set to work on their individual projects, he at the front of the barn and she near the back.

Eugenie considered the job before her. It seemed daunting but so had the pile of papers she used to have to go through for her father. The best strategy was to just dive in. Taking a deep breath, she got to work in one corner, her plan being to gradually make her way across the room, towards the door. With so many pieces of furniture sold, it had left an empty area where she could place items she believed were saleable. Those she felt were truly junk, she set in a pile for Ben to take to the recycling station.

After some time, she realized Ben was whistling softly. The sound made her smile; it was nice to be working companionably alongside someone. When she'd worked with her father at the university, the room had always been deadly silent except for when he'd bark an order at her.

Her stomach knotted as she recalled how quiet she'd tried to be, not wanting to disturb him. Every time she'd shifted in her seat, the creak of the straight-backed wooden chair would have him raising a brow at her. She'd whisper an apology and get back to work all the while wishing she dared jump up and go for a brisk walk.

She paused in her work and looked towards Ben. He wouldn't care if she announced she was going for a brisk walk. And he certainly didn't care how much noise she made; the tools he used filled the space with thumps and bangs that were louder than any sound she'd ever created. Yes, he was the complete antithesis to her father, of almost any male she'd ever known for that matter.

Her eyes drifted over Ben's form taking in his broad shoulders, the play of his muscles through his sweat-dampened shirt as he lifted a piece of wood. Even unconscious and in danger of hypothermia he had aroused her interest. Now, in good health…well, when he dropped a nail and bent over to get it, the fit of his worn jeans captured her attention and she had to force herself to look away. The man was definitely built.

Another peek in his direction showed him now running his hands over some carved detail he'd created. He caressed the wood, tracing the curves, stroking his fingers up and down the smooth spindles, before leaning forwards and blowing gently on the wood to remove a bit of sawdust. Her mouth grew dry as she watched him, somehow imagining it was her body, her skin, he was touching, his breath feathering her ear...

Her wayward thoughts had her fanning herself, her skin becoming heated from within.

"Warm today, isn't it? Here."

With a start, she realized Ben was standing in front of her, a bottle of water extended toward her.

"Thanks." She cleared her throat. "Yes, it does seem quite warm today."

"Unusual for this time of the year but we'll have snow before the week's end if the weather forecast is to be believed." He sat on the edge of a nearby table.

"Snow? I love snow! We never had much at home."

"And where is home for you?" He took a swig of water.

"I'm from England, originally."

"Right, you said the other day. I thought I heard a bit of an accent."

She laughed. "And I thought you had a bit of one!"

"It's all in your perspective, I guess." He cast a glance behind her. "Just like this stuff you're sorting through. To me, it's junk, but you seem to be finding treasure."

"Yes, there are lots of good pieces."

"Well, I appreciate your going through it for me." He took another drink of water.

"It's really not a hardship." She gave a one-shouldered shrug as she watched him drink, noting the cords in his neck as he tilted his head back. "I enjoy it, plus I get to watch you...er...watch you make furniture, that is. Were you always interested in being a carpenter?"

Thankfully, he didn't seem to notice her slip for he launched into an explanation of how he'd gone to school to study art but, it was an impractical career choice and so he'd turned to carpentry. His father had taught him the basics of the trade and then he'd worked for a small local construction company before eventually taking over the business.

"You own your own company?"

His face darkened. "Owned. Past tense. An accountant friend and I took over the company when the original owner retired. We specialized in building custom homes, I supervised the construction side and he managed the finances. But when my dad became ill, I spent a lot of my time taking care of him and my partner ran the business into the ground behind my back." He crushed the water bottle in his hand.

"I'm so sorry."

He stood, not acknowledging her sympathy. "Time to get back to work."

The companionable atmosphere between them dissipated like mist. He pitched the water bottle into the recycle bin with more force than necessary and quickly walked across the room to turn on the saw. The noise effectively ended the conversation.

She watched him for a moment before turning back to her sorting. She hadn't known he was an artist at heart. It made sense though. His work was exceptional, more than just boards hooked together to create furniture. It was an art form in itself, though she doubted he'd see it that way.

With a sigh, she continued her task. Old signs advertising gasoline for sale, rusted tools, broken furniture, a pair of ice skates, a cardboard box containing old gramophone recordings. She took some time to examine the thick, one-sided discs. None of the titles were familiar; her parents hadn't approved of listening to popular music. A collector, however, would definitely be interested in these, of that she was sure.

An old dollhouse caught her attention. It was stacked on a shelf, high overhead. She stood on her tiptoes and stretched but it remained just beyond her reach. Undaunted, she looked around and found an old wooden crate and dragged it over. It was a bit wobbly, however she didn't weigh that much.

Carefully, she stepped up and reached out for the dollhouse. Almost... She stretched a bit more, rising up on her toes. Her fingertips touched the corner and she began to ease it toward the edge.

"What the hell do you think you're doing?" Ben's voice boomed behind her.

She turned to look at him just as Chip decided it was the time to rush by barking at some unseen creature. As the dog brushed past her, she found herself falling. A cry of surprise escaped her and she closed her eyes, expecting to hit the ground but instead was encased in strong, warm arms. Looking up, she found her face extremely close to Ben's, her breasts pressed to his chest. She could feel the thumping of his heart, the light brush of his breath against her skin. Inhaling, she was struck by his scent, a fascinating mixture of man and fresh sawdust. Her mouth suddenly seeming dry, she licked her lips and slowly moved her gaze over his mouth up to his eyes. They were staring intently at her and she felt his grip tighten before he set her down with a decided thump.

"Next time you need to reach something, you ask for help." His voice was gruff as he moved away. "What were you trying to get?"

"There's an old dollhouse up there." She pointed towards the item on the shelf.

"Step back." He pushed a couple of boxes out of the way and easily reached the object, setting it down on a nearby table. "Here you go."

"Thank you." She began to examine the dollhouse. "This is so cute. A little dusty but still a nice piece."

"It was my mother's when she was a little girl. I remember her saying she was going to give it to her own daughter." He gave a sad smile. "She died giving birth to my sister."

"And the baby? She died, too?"

"Yeah." He took a deep breath. "It was just me and my dad after that."

She made no comment but secretly thought what a sad life he'd led. "I'm sure any little girl would have loved to have played with a toy like this. I know I would have."

"Why don't you keep it?"

"Me? Oh, no I couldn't. I'm sure you'd earn quite a bit from the sale of it."

"Money isn't everything." He shoved his hands in his pockets. "You're trying to help me and I'd like to be able to do something in return. It would make me feel better."

Michael had said something similar about money. Had the archangel known this conversation was coming? Sometimes she was sure he knew more than he let on.

She stared at the dollhouse once again, hesitating. "It *is* adorable and I always wanted one. My parents didn't believe in frivolous toys."

"So, you should have it." He reached out and gently moved one of the little doors, a sad smile passing over his lips. "I have no family to leave it to and I think my mom would have liked you."

"Well, thank you." Her mind raced. Was she allowed to accept gifts from a client? And what would happen to the dollhouse after the assignment was done? She'd have to consult the GA handbook. She was sure she'd read a rule in there about situations like this.

"You know what? I have some furniture I made that would fit in here."

"Um...I think your stuff is a bit too big."

He chuckled. "No. In my spare time, I make kids' toys. It's just a hobby. Come on, I'll show you."

Ben led the way to the house and she followed intrigued about this new side to the gruff man.

Ben pushed open the backdoor and walked through the kitchen, his step momentarily slowing. The disaster before him had him wincing. He hadn't cared about the state of the house for quite some time now. Life had been overwhelming for so long that he'd grown tired of fighting, tired of trying to pull himself up just to get kicked down before he'd regained his footing. With Eugenie in the room though, he was looking at the space with more critical eyes and wondering what she was thinking. Women were fussy about houses and even he knew the dirty dishes in the sink were gross.

"I keep meaning to clean the place up. Dad was never much of a housekeeper and when I moved in here after my divorce, well..."

"Things got out of hand."

"Yeah." He liked that she didn't criticize even though there were plenty of things she could have commented on.

As he made his way down the hall to the backroom where he did his carving, he began to question his decision to show her his work. His ex-wife had scoffed at his efforts, claiming he'd never make any money wasting his time on things like that. All she'd wanted was for him to work and bring home a pay cheque that she could spend. Their relationship had been a fire that had burned hot and bright only to be reduced to ashes within a short time.

Eugenie was different, he reminded himself. He was comfortable around her in a way he'd never been with Sabrina. Maybe that was why he was willing to share his hobby with her.

"I work in this spare bedroom." He flicked on the lights and then stepped aside so she could enter. There was a table in the centre of the room with his current projects and various tools. Along the walls were shelves displaying his finished pieces. Bowls, the wood polished to a high shine. Tiny beds, tables and chairs suitable for a dollhouse, trucks and cars, simple yet sturdy toys for a child to play with. And then there were the miniature animals and birds; he tried to make each one unique, spending hours refining the details that would add a lifelike quality to each piece.

"These are great!" Eugenie's eyes lit up as she examined the items on the shelves. "Any child would love to play with them."

"I like kids," he confessed, watching her reaction to his words.

"Me, too." Eugenie turned each piece over in her hands. Her appreciation of the work was evident in the way she tested the wheels, or carefully worked the delicate hinges.

"I started working on these years ago. Growing up with just my dad and me, I'd always planned on a big family but..." His voice trailed off at that painful thought. Sabrina hadn't wanted kids. Had in fact been happy when they hadn't conceived. He'd wasted so many years trying to make her happy. Suddenly the room felt too stuffy, as if the very thought of her was squeezing the life out of him. "I have to go."

Abruptly, he turned and left the room, only vaguely aware of Eugenie staring after him in surprise.

He walked out of the house and stood in the middle of the yard. The bleakness of November surrounded him; barren trees, no birds singing. The tall wild grasses and flowers that grew along the roadside were dead and brown, rustling sadly in the cold wind. Even the sun that had shone brightly earlier in the day was gone, hidden behind the dark grey clouds that heralded a change in the weather. It matched the feeling inside him.

He took a deep breath and glanced back at the house. Eugenie must think he was crazy running out like that but...he shook his head. He couldn't go back in that room right now. Those toys represented dreams that had never come true. Never would, either. He'd not trust his heart to another woman. Instead he whistled for Chip and set off for a brisk walk down the lane that twisted its way behind his house and led into the small wooded area on the edge of the property.

Chapter 6

Eugenie peered out the window, watching Ben head off to who knows where. At least he had the dog with him for company and hopefully he'd stay away from that rickety bridge. And, if anything should happen to him again, she was confident Chip would come and get her. However, she was worried about more than just his physical well-being. She sensed a loneliness inside him, a deep hurt.

She placed the small train she'd been looking at back on the shelf. Being in his private room while he was away didn't seem right so she turned off the light and closed the door, though not before she'd noticed something large in the corner draped with a cloth. Her curiosity was piqued by the shrouded object and she took a step closer before deciding against uncovering it. If Ben had wanted her to see whatever was under the cloth, he'd have shown it to her.

Feeling awkward in the house by herself, she intended to go back to work in the barn but slowed as she passed through the kitchen. It really was desperately in need of cleaning. She was surprised Ben didn't get sick with food poisoning.

Despite the fact she'd done no real cleaning in her earthly life, she couldn't resist tackling the dishes. Plus, it was the one job she felt confident doing. A grimace passed over her face as she drained the cold, greasy water. Hot water and the liberal use of dish soap would deal with the problem though.

She washed the plates, bowls and cups, then scoured the collection of pans. When she came upon a shot glass, she paused. Ben had been drinking that first day but since then he'd been sober, or at least only imbibing lightly. That was a positive change. When she dried the dishes and put them away, she made sure to tuck the shot glass towards the back; out of sight, out of mind.

Once the dishes were done she decided to wipe down the counters. Unfortunately, the stove was still dirty, the floor needed mopping and the curtains were laden with dust, not to mention you could barely see out the windows. There was no way she'd have time to get everything done unless...

Zeke had explained she likely had powers she hadn't discovered yet. Maybe this was the time to start exploring them. The trick was to coordinate thought and gesture, or so Zeke had told her. She decided to start with cleaning the floor. Hand out, palm down, she furrowed her brow imagining water covering the floor, a mop swishing it about to lift the grime. Before her eyes a sheen of water did appear on the floor but...bloody hell...too much!

"No! Stop! Enough!" She felt like the inept sorcerer's apprentice in the poem by Goethe, shouting instructions.

By the time she'd regained control, the floor was clean but her shoes were wet and squished with each step. Grumbling, she sat down and removed them, placing them near the furnace vent to dry. Well, at least she had a clean floor to walk on now.

Using a chair, she took down the curtains next and placed them in the sink; the washing machine looked far too complicated for her to try. She flicked her wrist and thought about soap and sure enough some appeared in the sink. Was it enough though? The curtains were really quite filthy. Maybe just a tad more. When a nice puddle of soap was in the sink, she turned on the taps and watched with a pleased smile as bubbles began to appear. Satisfied, she left the curtains sloshing about in the water and turned to the stove.

Removing the grease from it proved to be a snap, a scrubber zipping over the surface at blinding speed. She gave a nod of approval and glanced back to see how the curtains were doing only to give a cry of horror. Soap bubbles were spilling over the edge of the sink and dripping down the cupboard doors.

At least she didn't panic this time and managed to handle the situation without too many more mishaps. She did decide, however, to avoid using her powers on anything that involved water and used good old-fashioned elbow grease to clean the windows while the curtains dripped dry on a rack in the laundry room.

With the kitchen finally cleaned, she looked in the fridge. It appeared Ben had purchased groceries recently. It would be nice for him to come home to a hot meal except, of course, she had no idea how to cook.

"Zeke?" She called out his name and before she could blink he appeared beside her.

"What's up, Babe? Michael's given me a really important assignment so I can't spare a lot of time."

"I need to cook a meal and I haven't the faintest idea how to go about it.

"Let's see what we've got, shall we?" He started opening cabinets and peered into the refrigerator. "Okay, how long do we have?"

"I've no idea. Ben stomped out with his dog. Something I said really upset him."

"Okay. Well, you've got the ingredients for pasta and Bolognese sauce which, by the way, is my favourite so I'm going to show you how to make it and then one day you can invite me over for dinner."

Zeke surprised her by giving her very easy to follow instructions, allowing her to do the cooking while he supervised. It wasn't long before the sauce was gently simmering and the pasta draining.

"Now all you need is a small side salad and you're all set." He removed some vegetables from the fridge and showed her how to wash and cut them. "I don't see any dressing but there's the olive oil we used earlier. Leave it on the table and he can help himself if he wants some."

"Thank you, Zeke!" Eugenie threw her arms around her colleague and hugged him, only to back away feeling embarrassed. She'd never done anything like that before. Was this easy feeling she had around Zeke what she had witnessed between Annie and her brother all those years ago?

Zeke didn't appear to notice her awkwardness. In fact, he went a little pink but grinned at her. "Have fun with your man."

"Oh, but he's not my..." But Zeke had already left and she was alone in the kitchen.

The meal prepared, she surveyed her afternoon's work. Dinner was simmering on the stove, the table was set for one, the kitchen was clean and tidy. She gave a satisfied smile and was preparing to leave when she heard the backdoor opening.

"Whoa! What happened in here?" Ben pushed the door shut, blocking the cool breeze that had followed him inside through the utility room. His cheeks were reddened from the cold, his hair wind-swept. Chip had come in with him and immediately made his way to a bowl of dog food that stood in the corner.

"I...I hope you don't mind." She watched his eyes sweep over the kitchen and began to feel nervous. Had she overstepped herself? "I know it was presumptuous of me. I'd only intended to do the dishes but then one thing led to another and..." She ended with a shrug.

"No. I don't mind." He turned in a slow circle. "I don't mind at all. I haven't seen the kitchen look this good since, well, I guess back when I was a kid."

"I made you dinner, too. I figured you'd be tired and hungry by the time you got home."

He walked over to the stove, lifted the lid and gave an experimental sniff. "This smells great."

"Well, I hope you enjoy it." She walked towards the door. "I'll be back tomorrow morning to continue working in the barn."

"Where are you going? Since you've gone to the trouble of making dinner, you should at least stay and have some."

"I made it for you. I—"

"Nonsense." He placed his hand in the small of her back and guided her away from the door. "I'll go wash up. Set yourself a place at the table. No arguing." He raised a brow at her and she found herself conceding.

The meal was delicious, even if she did say so herself. Casual conversation flowed between them. She spoke of her life growing up in England, trying to keep her comments general enough that the passage of nearly a century wouldn't be noticed. It was interesting that they'd both been only children. His father, however, had always been warm and caring.

"Yeah, even after my mom died, Dad always tried his best to make sure I had a good home life. He made cookies for school bake sales, helped me create Halloween costumes. And every year we'd go and get a Christmas tree together."

"It sounds like you have some great memories."

Ben nodded and then pushed his chair back. "That was a great meal. Thanks. I'll gather up the plates while you relax."

"No. No need. I'm here to help."

"Help clear out the barn," he reminded her. "Not act as my maid."

"How about we do them together then?" She picked up her plate and walked to the sink without waiting for his answer.

They stood side by side at the sink. Ben washed while she rinsed. He towered over her but his height didn't make her feel her lack of inches. Funny how she'd never liked being short and often felt intimidated around tall people. But with Ben she felt safe, protected, even though she had to tip her head back to look at him.

Occasionally, their arms brushed, fingers touching as they passed the dishes. It made her feel warm inside. Different, confused and yet, wishing the contact could be repeated. She found herself working slower, trying to drag the chore out but eventually the dishes were done and she could delay no longer.

"I need to be heading home." She folded the dish towel and hung it up.

"It's dark outside." Ben pointed out. "You can't walk to the bus stop in the dark."

"I'll be fine." Her plan was that as soon as she was outside and out of sight from the house, she'd dematerialize and pop back to her apartment. He didn't know that, of course.

"Nonsense. I'm driving you home. A man doesn't let a woman walk in the dark by herself. I'll just grab my keys."

In no time at all she was in Ben's truck and he was driving her home. It was a cool night, her breath showing like little puffs of white mist as she breathed. He flicked on the heater and she relaxed in the seat as the warm air flowed over her.

Looking out the window, she could see the stars twinkling in the night sky as the moon shone brightly. Frost made the tree branches glisten, and in the fields she could see the shadowy shapes of deer emerging from the woods to feed on the bits of grain left behind after the harvest.

All too soon they arrived at her apartment. Ben turned off the engine and silence filled the small space.

She cleared her throat. "Thanks for the ride."

"No problem." He was watching her, his eyes skimming over her features.

She felt her heartbeat quicken, the atmosphere between them growing thick. Unsure of what was coming, she fumbled with her seatbelt but it didn't seem to want to release.

"Let me." Ben leaned closer, easily releasing the mechanism.

He was so close she could make out the stubble on his chin in the dim light of the dashboard dials, see the curve of his mouth, the long lashes that surrounded his green eyes. And then he was leaning closer. His mouth brushed over hers once, twice and then he moved away. His hand reached up and skimmed over her cheek, tucking a strand of hair behind her ear, his eyes fixed on hers.

"Thanks again, Eugenie. I enjoyed the dinner."

"You're welcome." Her voice came out breathily as if she'd been running and it did indeed feel that way. His kiss had set her heart pounding. Reluctantly, she opened the door.

"I'll wait until you're inside. Be sure to lock up."

"I will."

She hurried from the truck and raced up the stairs, turning when she reached the top. He was still watching her. It made her feel incredibly cared for, even cherished. With a quick wave, she unlocked the door and stepped into her apartment. Leaning against the wall, she pressed her hands to her warm face. She'd never known a GA assignment could be like this!

Ben watched as Eugenie shut her door and a light went on inside her apartment. Once he was sure she was safely inside, he started the engine and headed home.

His fingers tightened on the steering wheel as he considered the fact that he'd kissed her. Why had he done that? He'd not planned on it and yet it had suddenly seemed the right thing to do. Her scent had wrapped around him, the warmth of her breath skimming over his face.

That brief taste of her had been exquisite and he'd had to force himself not to deepen the kiss. He sensed her inexperience. There was something about her that seemed pure and innocent. She wasn't the kind you messed around with casually. And there was the crux of the problem. He had no intention of having a serious relationship with anyone. That being the case, he'd best keep his distance from young Eugenie Winslow. Yep, no more companionable dinners, no more moonlight rides. It was the right thing to do.

Too bad the right thing seemed to suck.

Chapter 7

Eugenie brushed the curtains aside and watched Ben drive away. He'd kissed her. She still couldn't believe it. It had been...well...she wasn't sure how to describe it. The delicious tingle that had shot through her when their lips had touched, the heat of his body so close to hers. His hand as it had brushed her cheek had been work-roughened, stimulating her nerve endings, making her overly aware of his presence. And his eyes, staring into hers, she could easily have become lost in their deep forest green.

Her experience with men was almost non-existent. The encounter with Jonathan on the night before she died was really all she had to go by. It had shown just how little she knew about men. In her naiveté, she had imagined all kinds of scenarios the night after that art show, not one of them had included his wife and child. But Ben... Ben had kissed her lips. There was no misunderstanding that!

But, Ben was a client. Michael had told her to interact with him however she was sure he hadn't meant starting a physical relationship...or had he? Maybe she should visit Michael and get some clarification.

With a thought, she transported herself to the waiting area outside Michael's office. The room was empty, the lighting dim. No one was at the reception desk. In fact, even the hallways appeared to be devoid of occupants. She bit her lip. A glance at the clock on the wall revealed it was quite late. Was Michael even here?

A thin line of light showed under his door so she gathered her courage and tentatively tapped at the door.

There was a moment of silence and then the sound of footsteps approaching.

"Yes?" Michael's gaze stared out over her head then lowered, his eyes widening when he saw her. "Eugenie?"

"Hello, sir. I'm sorry to arrive unannounced. I realize it's quite late—"

He held up a hand. "No rambling, remember?" Taking a step to the side, he ushered her in. "What brings you here this late at night?"

"I have a question about my assignment."

"I see. Well, take a seat." He walked to his desk and sat down.

Eugenie noticed all the papers and files before him, the weary slump to his shoulders, the tired shadows under his eyes. His hair was mussed as if he'd been running his fingers through it and there was even stubble on his chin. One part of her brain noted he was darkly handsome while another part focused on the fact that she'd never stopped to consider when Michael did his work. Whenever she'd been in his office, his desk had always been clean save for a few carefully aligned folders.

"Eugenie?" He drew her attention back to him. "As you can see I still have considerable work to complete. If you need something...?"

"I'm sorry." She clasped her hands in her lap. "My client kissed me tonight." Then she gasped. She hadn't meant to blurt out that fact in quite such a blunt manner.

"Really?" Michael leaned back in his chair, his hand stroking his chin. Was there a hint of a smile there? "And that concerns you?"

"Yes. I'm not sure what to do."

"Did you enjoy the kiss?"

"It was wonderful!" She paused and furrowed her brow. "But is it allowed? I don't want to break the rules. And he offered me a gift. His mother's dollhouse from when she was a child. I'm sure I read somewhere that a guardian angel shouldn't accept favours from a client."

"The exact wording is that *a GA cannot coerce a client into offering either material or physical favours*. Our clients are often emotionally vulnerable and we can't take advantage of them. However, if they are initiating the interactions, it's another matter. To refuse a gift, freely given, would not only be rude but could damage the relationship."

Eugenie nodded. "I understand."

"The GA has to consider the mental and emotional state of the client. If they are of sound mind, if the bestowing of the gift will contribute to the client finding their way, then the GA is free to proceed."

"Ben is of sound mind. As to whether giving me something of his mother's will help in any way—"

Michael interrupted, leaning forward, his hands clasped on the desktop, "Eugenie, I feel you are overthinking. 'Go with your gut' as I've heard some say. You have good instincts and a loving heart. Remember you were chosen for this job for a reason and it wasn't because there were doubts as to your ability."

"Okay. Thank you." She stood. "I'm sorry to have bothered you."

"You're never a bother, Eugenie. It's more like you are a breath of fresh air."

Flustered at the compliment, she gave a half shrug. "I'm just me. Nothing special."

"I beg to differ, but I'll leave it for now."

As she turned to leave, she noticed Michael rolling his shoulders before bending over his papers again. She hesitated. "Michael?"

"Yes?" He looked up. There was no denying his weariness.

"Is there anything I can do to help?" She gestured towards the papers on his desk. "You seem to have a lot to do but you look tired."

He smiled. "As I said, you have a tender heart. Don't worry, I'll get this done in a few hours."

"Isn't there anyone waiting at home for you?" She cocked her head, never having thought about Michael's life beyond the walls of this building.

"No, Eugenie. No one is waiting for me."

"Oh." Did she detect loneliness in his voice? Was this job all he had in his life?

He shook his head. "I can see the wheels turning in your head, Eugenie. I'm not one of your clients. I'm perfectly fine. Now go back to that apartment you rented and get some rest. I'm sure you'll have a busy day tomorrow."

"All right." She'd been dismissed... In the nicest of ways, of course, but dismissed nonetheless. Poor Michael. So much work to do and all alone. Giving her head a sad shake, she headed back to her apartment.

That night she dreamed of overtired archangels who nodded in approval as a gruff carpenter held her close and kissed her senseless.

Someone was hammering. Was she still dreaming about Ben? Experimentally, she opened her eyes and saw the ceiling in her bedroom. No, it wasn't Ben. It sounded like someone was trying to break down her front door. After grabbing her robe and pushing her arms into the garment, she went to see what all the fuss was about. A glance through the peep hole in the apartment door revealed Zeke waiting on the other side. She opened the door, a puzzled frown on her face.

"Zeke! What are you doing here? Aren't you on assignment?"

"Yeah, but it's mostly night work. I grabbed a couple hours of shut-eye and then picked this up for you." He held up what looked like a slim book.

"What's that?"

"It's a tablet. You've seen them around, I'm sure; I know Michael has one. I thought you could make use of a computer. This is pretty powerful and you can do most things on it that you can on a regular laptop.

"But, Zeke, I haven't a clue how to use such a thing."

"Oh ye of little faith! I'm numero uno when it comes to knowing all things tech. Let's pretend we're human and make some coffee and I'll teach you all you need to know about the wonders of the internet while you eat breakfast."

"Perfect! You can also show me how to use the microwave!"

A few hours later, Eugenie arrived at Ben's place with her new tablet tucked under her arm. It was mid-morning and Ben was already at work sanding the surface of a board. For a moment, she paused to admire the play of muscles as he worked before giving her head a shake and announcing her presence.

"Good morning, Ben." She raised her voice so as to be heard over the sound of the power tool.

He looked over his shoulder at her and nodded then returned to work.

Surprised, she stared at his back. After his kiss last night, she'd expected more. Nothing major like him declaring undying devotion, but something. A smile, a hint of warmth, a good morning kiss?

She pressed her lips together. Had she misunderstood his actions? From what she'd observed on the television Zeke had given her, kissing was far more common and carried less meaning than it had in her day but somehow she'd felt Ben was different. Perhaps she'd been wrong.

Not knowing what else to do, she headed to the rear of the barn and resumed her work. Using her tablet, she began to take pictures of the items she'd already sorted, planning on researching them later to determine their value. This thing called the internet that Zeke had shown her truly was a wealth of information.

Eventually, she became lost in her work and gave a start when the sound of voices finally intruded on her thoughts. Looking up, she realized Ben had customers. Angelic customers.

It was important to maintain her story that she'd asked friends to check out Ben's furniture, so she made a point of noticing them.

"Hello, thanks for stopping by." She called out the greeting as she walked over to where they stood admiring a set of shelves.

"Hi Eugenie! We heard you'd been praising this furniture and you were right. His work is superb." Carmen, one of the angels, ran her hand over some of the carved detailing before moving on to look at another piece.

"One of your friends?" Ben asked in a lowered voice.

"Yes, we...er...used to live in the same neighbourhood." Eugenie felt that was close to the truth.

Ben nodded and then went to answer a query from one of the other angels.

After a few minutes, she went back to work while keeping an eye on Ben and his customers. It appeared they'd purchased a few pieces and placed an order for more. She held back a smile, pleased her plan was helping Ben get back on his feet.

When the transactions were complete, Ben came to speak to her.

"Eugenie, you're a miracle worker. I can't believe you know so many people who need furniture. This group has just opened a small bed and breakfast and want some unique pieces—" He stopped and gave a soft laugh. "But I guess you know that if they're friends of yours."

"Right." A twinge of guilt washed over her at the white lie.

Thankfully, Ben changed the topic as he glanced at his watch. "It's almost noon. Would you like to share a pizza with me? It's just frozen, though."

"Sure. I'd love to." His offer had her smiling.

"I'll go put it in the oven and give you a call when it's ready."

"Thanks. I'll get some more of this stuff catalogued."

With a nod, Ben headed for the house and she watched him leave, a flutter of excitement filling her.

Ben took the pizza out of the oven. The cheese was bubbling, the crust lightly browned. Perfect. It would be cool enough to eat by the time Eugenie walked up to the house.

"Okay, Chip, go get our guest." He opened the door and the old dog gave a happy woof before running towards the barn. Hopefully, Eugenie would understand Chip was trying to get her to come inside.

After taking plates from the cupboard, he went looking around for napkins. Usually, he'd grab a paper towel but women were fancier than that. He began to pull open drawers and cupboards wondering where the hell napkins might be only to pause and run a hand through his hair. What was he doing? He wasn't worried about impressing Eugenie. They were sharing a frozen pizza. It was a simple thank you for the customers she'd sent his way.

He took a deep breath and slowly exhaled. This was exactly what he'd told himself he wouldn't do. When Eugenie had greeted him this morning, he'd been purposely cool. He'd sensed her behind him, watching him, confused over his apparent dismissal of her but he hadn't wanted to lead her on. They were friends, barely more than acquaintances. The kiss had been a mistake, an anomaly.

Right.

He looked at the drawers he'd pulled open in his search and pushed them shut. No napkins, no extra fuss.

"Ben?"

He turned at the sound of Eugenie's voice.

"Chip was barking and kept running this way and looking at me so I assumed you'd sent him to tell me lunch was ready."

"You were right. I just took the pizza out of the oven."

"Great." She stepped inside and took off her coat.

He noticed the tip of her nose was pink and so were her cheeks. The temperature was dropping steadily, the predicted cold front finally arriving.

"I'll just set my coat here." She laid it on a chair and with a start Ben realized he'd been staring at her.

"Yeah. That's good." He turned and pulled open the fridge door. "What would you like to drink? I have soda—"

"Just water will be fine." She stepped towards the cupboards and took out a glass. He noticed her pause, her eyes seeming to settle on the shot glass that sat on the counter.

Last night, after taking her home, he'd come home intending to take a drink or two in order to rid himself of all thoughts of women but, at the last minute he'd changed his mind. For some reason, drinking himself into oblivion hadn't been appealing and he'd gone to bed stone cold sober. Of course, Eugenie wouldn't know that. He braced himself for a snide comment about drinking too much but instead she merely continued on to fill her glass with water.

Ben watched as she completed the simple task. Sabrina would have nagged. Hell, Sabrina wouldn't even have settled for tap water. She'd have wanted some fancy carbonated kind, at the very least. As a matter of fact, she would never have accepted his offer of frozen pizza. He scowled at how many years he'd wasted.

"Ben? Are you all right?"

He gave himself a mental shake. "Yeah, just thinking about something."

"Oh." Eugenie picked up the tray with the pizza and set it on the table.

The fact she didn't start asking him questions was a surprise. It was a pleasant change. Sabrina had loved to hear all the dirty details. Pushing thoughts of his ex out of his mind, he grabbed a soda for himself and sat down opposite Eugenie at the small kitchen table.

"This is good,' she commented as she licked a bit of sauce from her fingers.

He watched the action, fascinated by the way her tongue slipped out between her lips. It caused a reaction in his body and he shifted in his chair, fumbling for something to say. "Sorry, I couldn't find any napkins." He immediately regretted it. Why was he pointing that out?

"I'm fine." She smiled at him then took another bite of her pizza, laughing at the cheese string that formed.

Chapter 8

Lunch somehow progressed to Ben showing her around the house. It had been in his family since the 1940s, purchased by his grandfather shortly after returning home from the war. Apparently, he'd met Ben's grandmother while he was in England prior to the D-Day landings, married her and had brought her back to Canada after the war.

"I love these dishes." Eugenie paused in front of a curio cabinet that displayed some fine china.

"My grandmother's. She brought them over with her." Ben stood behind her and she could see his reflection in the glass. "There are a few other things in the house that were hers as well."

"Really? What else?"

"Well, there's this lamp." He gestured towards the item and Eugenie struggled not to make a face. It was truly hideous.

"That's…er…interesting."

Ben laughed. "You can say that again. It's as ugly as sin. Apparently, my grandfather kept threatening to throw it out every time they had an argument."

"I'm surprised he didn't get rid of it even if they weren't arguing."

"I guess he had great self-restraint." Ben guided her to the living room. "Just to prove my grandmother's family didn't have completely dreadful taste, check out this painting." His hands on her shoulders, Ben turned her to face a painting…of herself!

"That's really lovely!" She gaped at the artwork, an icy wave washing over her. It was the painting Jonathan had done of her the night before she'd died. Well, not exactly. This was the finished article and far more detailed than the half-done product she'd seen.

Her throat felt tight and it was difficult to swallow as she recalled that evening. She'd been deceived by the dashing artist, or had she deceived herself. Whatever the case, it was because him that she'd been in such a daze the following morning until Annabelle had shattered her dreams by announcing he was married. If it hadn't been for that, she might have seen the truck coming, she might have…

'What ifs' flew through her head and it took her a moment to realize Ben was still talking. He hadn't appeared to notice her reaction.

"Yes, my great-grandfather, an aspiring artist, painted this but he never sold it."

She raised a shaking hand to her throat, struggling to keep her voice calm. "Any idea why?"

"Family legend has it the girl who sat for it was killed soon after. All we know beyond that is he refused to sell it."

"That's quite the…er…story."

"It is, isn't it?" Ben stepped closer to the picture, his hands clasped behind his back. "It's always fascinated me. Both the story and this painting. I've often wondered about the girl. Her smile, the expression in her eyes. There's an innocence there, a trace of sadness, longing..." His voice trailed off.

Eugenie suddenly blinked, a horrible thought occurring to her. What if Ben realized she was the girl in the painting? True, her hair was different as was her clothing but… Did Michael know about this? She needed to get out of here and fast!

"Ben, I just remembered I…er…I have an appointment and I'm going to be late. Sorry, but I need to leave now." She backed away, heading toward the door.

"I can give you a ride." Ben turned towards her and she ducked her head so her hair fell forward partially hiding her face, not caring that he'd probably wonder what she was doing.

"No. It's fine. You need to finish that chair you're working on. I'll talk to you later!" And with that, she grabbed her coat and dashed out the door.

Ben watched Eugenie leave. Through the window, he could see her hurrying down the lane, hands tucked in her pockets, shoulders hunched against the cold. For a moment, he considered following her. It wouldn't take any time to catch up to her in the truck. He jingled the keys in his pocket and then shook his head.

He'd offered. She'd already refused. Going after her wasn't a good idea. He'd been down that road with his ex. At first Sabrina had done everything she could to get his attention and then, once he was interested, she'd started blowing hot and cold and he'd ended up doing all the chasing. She'd been like that pretty unattainable bauble you'd try to win at a fair. He'd done everything he could to get her attention and convince her to marry him. When he'd finally won her over, it turned out she'd not been worth the effort.

He glanced out the window one more time and then turned away. He'd not make the same mistake again. He wouldn't push for a relationship with Eugenie. Not that she was anything like Sabrina. No, Eugenie seemed sweet and caring and helpful, the kind of woman he should have gone after the first time round, the kind his dad had said he should find. Too bad he hadn't listened. It was too late now, though. No more relationships for him. He had nothing left to offer beyond a quick roll in the hay and that wasn't good enough for a woman like Eugenie.

He stared at the painting again and then cocked his head. The woman in the painting bore a striking resemblance to her. The hair was different of course but... No, it was a coincidence. The woman in the painting had been dead for almost a hundred years.

His eyes trailed over the image and then he headed towards the back bedroom feeling inspired. In the corner, draped with a cloth was a carving he'd begun working on years ago. It was a bust, a head and shoulders carving of the woman in the painting but he'd never finished it. Every time he sat down to work on it, he'd end up staring at it not sure what to do next. It was good but it was inanimate; lacking a certain spark that would take it from good to amazing. Today was different though. Today, he just knew what needed to be done to bring the carving to life.

Gathering his tools, he began to work.

Michael looked up from his computer screen. Someone was tapping at his door but he had no meetings scheduled. He cast his mind over the various GAs and the assignments they were on. The only one that caused him concern was Zeke. The GA was on a case as well as helping Eugenie. Hopefully, the lad wasn't over-extending himself. Zeke had come a long way in the past year; offering to mentor Eugenie spoke well of his character. Yes, the boy had a lot of potential…provided he didn't get carried away and do something crazy beyond his skill level!

He sighed and logged out of the file he'd been perusing and leaned back in his chair. Whoever was out there was still waiting. "Enter."

The door cracked open and Eugenie poked her head in. "I'm sorry to bother you again, sir, but do you have a minute?"

Ah, Eugenie. He should have known. She was so excited about her assignment and seemed to need extra assurance. He really ought to have had her take those training courses rather than studying the rule book but at the time he hadn't foreseen her going out on her own quite so soon. Her own actions had precipitated her current course though and now all he could do was give her guidance.

"Come in. Have a seat." He nodded towards the chair across from him and she slid into it. As always, her hands were neatly folded in her lap, her knees pressed together, her back straight. Would she ever lose that quaint properness? "What can I do for you?"

"Sir, I just discovered that Ben, my client, has a picture of me!"

Michael quirked a brow. "I fail to see the problem."

"It's a portrait. His great grandfather painted me when I was alive, back in 1923. What if Ben recognizes me?"

"A guardian angel has to be able to think on his, or her, feet."

"I know but—"

He shook his head and leaned back in his chair, steepling his fingers. "I'm not going to solve this for you, Eugenie. Yes, it could become an issue, but you can handle it."

"Oh." She wrinkled her brow, seeming deep in thought. "I suppose I could say it was an odd coincidence."

"You could."

"Or suggest I might be a distant relative of the person in the portrait. That would be plausible since he knows I'm from England."

"Excellent idea." He smiled at her. "And if all else fails you could perform a mind wipe."

She paled and he struggled to keep a smile from his face. New guardian angels were required to take a crash course in emergency mind wipes in case they were ever detected. The instructor was a long-suffering elderly angel who was constantly looking for volunteers willing to have minor memories, such as the last movie they watched, erased from their minds. By time the lessons were complete, the volunteers often had a stunned look, having been subjected to multiple inept attempts at mind wipes. They seldom volunteered again but the young GAs left the course properly prepared for their job. Eugenie had passed the course…barely…and the idea of performing a real mind wipe on a human obviously didn't sit well with her.

She cleared her throat. "That sounds rather extreme. I know how to do targeted mind wipes but I've never performed a full one before. What if I remove too much of his memory? What if he forgets who I am?"

"Eventually that will have to happen." He watched her expression, noting the look of surprise followed by sadness. It would seem the girl was becoming attached to her client. Not unusual given the circumstances and an occupational hazard, especially for the young ones. "Eugenie, you know that's how it works. Once an assignment is done, the client's mind is wiped removing all traces of you from their memory and replacing it with a plausible explanation for any changes that have occurred."

She wet her lips. "I'd forgotten that part."

"Is this going to be a problem for you? Do you need to be removed from the assignment?"

"No! Please sir. I don't want to quit." Her eyes widened in alarm and she leaned forward as she pressed her point. "This is my first job with interaction and I want to see it through."

"Very well. As long as you don't make the mistake of trying to guard your heart at the expense of helping your client."

"I won't, sir." She nodded but he could see the worry she was trying to hide. Her heart was tender, untried. Had she really understood that the heart of a guardian angel often bled before an assignment was over? It was the price they had to pay if they wanted the satisfaction of a job well done.

As she hurried from the office, Michael narrowed his eyes. The next few weeks should prove to be interesting;

the young GA's future rested in her own hands. He returned to the file he'd been reading on his computer but not before he wondered which path Eugenie would take.

Ben arched his back. He'd been working for hours on the carving, adding subtle details to the curve of the mouth, the angle of the jaw. Turning it slowly, he gave it a critical look. It was good. Very good. And it bore an uncanny resemblance to Eugenie. Hadn't she said she'd been raised in England? It would be an incredible coincidence if she was related to the woman in the portrait.

He glanced at the time. It was late and he'd not finished the rocking chair. Damn. Well then, he'd have to get up extra early in the morning. The light in the barn wasn't suitable for working at night. If he ever had the funds, he'd love to build a new barn and outfit it as a proper wood-working shop. Not that that was very likely. It would be years before he could pay off his debts and have any spare cash-flow.

With a sigh, he tidied up his work area and then headed outside. He needed to make sure the old stove in the barn was off and the door was locked. There wasn't much crime in the area but he didn't want to chance having his tools stolen.

As he passed through the kitchen he noticed the dirty dishes from lunch still on the table. Their surfaces were suspiciously clean and there was no left-over pizza on the tray. A glance toward the corner where Chip was resting had him narrowing his eyes suspiciously.

"Did you help yourself to the pizza and then lick off the plates?

Chip raised his head and then burped loudly.

"You just incriminated yourself. You realize that, don't you?"

Chip thumped his tail and gave a low woof.

"Well, at least you're honest. I can't abide people who keep secrets."

Making a mental note to wash the plates with extra hot water, he headed out to close up the shop for the night.

Chapter 9

Eugenie stood by the window, her chin in her palm, her elbows on the window ledge as she watched the snow coming down. A short while ago the flakes had been sporadic, twirling and dancing to some silent melody before lightly landing on the ground to join their kin. The wind had since picked up and a thick blanket of snow now covered the yard around Ben's workshop. When she'd arrived this morning, the sky had been grey, a distinctive nip in the air in contrast to the warmer temperatures of the previous few days.

"It's going to snow today," Ben had announced when she'd commented about the change.

"That's wonderful." The news had had her grinning while Ben had laughed shaking his head.

"I remember my mother loved the snow. She used to tell me the angels were having a pillow fight and that was where the snowflakes come from."

"Angels don't..." She'd caught herself and coughed. "I'm mean that's a cute story."

"Yeah." His eyes had grown distant as if caught up in a memory and then he gave a shrug. "I'd better get back to work. I'm behind schedule on this chair."

She'd nodded and made her way back to her own work area.

That had been several hours ago. Now drifts were forming across the driveway, the snow falling thick and fast, the whirl of white mesmerizing. When a pair of warm hands cupped her shoulders, she gave a start of surprise.

"It's really coming down out there." Ben's voice sounded near her ear and she looked up to see him frowning at the weather. "I was so busy working I wasn't watching the weather. I'd better get you home before the roads are impassable."

"Okay."

"Head up to the house with Chip. I'm going to shut things down out here and then see how deep the snow is in the driveway."

Eugenie heeded his instructions and followed Chip who was plowing a pathway through the drifts, barking in excitement. She stumbled a few times, once completely losing her footing and landing in the snow on her back staring up at the sky. Chip ambled over to check on her, nudging her with his wet nose. Laughing, she pushed him away before clambering to her feet.

By the time she was in the house, both she and the dog were covered in snow. She brushed as much off as she could, stomping her feet as she entered the house. Beside her, Chip shook himself free of snow, the water droplets flying from his fur spattering the walls as well as her.

"Thank you, Chip. As if I wasn't wet enough already." She wiped her face and he gave one more shake before making his way to his bed in the corner.

Eugenie took off her jacket and then plucked at her now wet pants. The wardrobe Zeke had helped her pick out wasn't made for this kind of weather. Her coat was too light, her boots too low and she hadn't thought of a hat or gloves. She pushed her wet hair from her face and wiggled her toes. Her socks were soaked and her feet felt like ice cubes. Zeke had explained, when she'd complained of the cold, that although at the moment she suffered from extremes of temperature, as she matured as a GA she would become immune to changes in the weather. But for the time being she had to be careful, because she could cause herself to become weak and disoriented if she succumbed to hypothermia or severe heat stress. In dire cases, he'd heard of new GAs actually fading away to nothing! She certainly didn't want that to happen; Ben needed her!

A hot cup of tea would help, so she put the kettle on, then peered out the window to watch Ben. He'd made it to the road and retrieved his mail and was now making his way back to the house. The snow seemed to be getting deeper by the minute, at times the wind whipping the flakes by so quickly she could barely see him.

"Sorry, Eugenie, but there's no way we can chance driving in this." Ben made the announcement as he entered the house, pushing against the wind to shut the door. "It's turning into a regular blizzard out there."

"You mean we're snowed in?" She glanced outside again.

"Yep. We'd be risking our lives trying to drive in this."

"Oh." The implications of being snowed in with Ben began to make themselves clear and she was almost ashamed to admit it sent a thrill through her.

The kettle began to whistle, so she bustled about adding water to the teapot and finding cups while Ben hung up his coat. The shot glass was back in the cupboard and she smiled at the knowledge Ben hadn't been imbibing. She had nothing against the occasional drink of alcohol as long as it wasn't used as an escape from one's problems.

"Here you go." She placed a steaming mug on the table.

"Thanks." He sat down, wrapping his hands around the vessel as if trying to absorb the warmth.

"I thought it would help ward off the chill."

They sat quietly, savouring the brew until practicalities had to be dealt with. Together they prepared a hot meal, working companionably within the confines of the small kitchen. Conversation centred around cooking and eating for most of the meal until an uneasy silence settled on the kitchen. Ben was studying her, frowning and then looking away. What was he thinking?

Her own thoughts, she knew, were in a turmoil. Thoughts of kisses and paintings swirled around in her mind mixing up with Ben's financial woes and her own inexperience of how to help him without exposing her Heavenly purpose. Suddenly, her mental meanderings were halted by Ben clearing his throat.

"I worked on a sculpture last night after you left."

"A sculpture? In wood?" She blinked not having expected him to mention his artwork.

"Yes. Remember that painting I showed you before you had to leave for an appointment?"

Eugenie lowered her eyes to hide her nervousness about him connecting the picture with her and nodded.

"It's always fascinated me. The family legend behind it. The girl's smile, the look in her eyes. Years ago, I even started to try to carve the girl's likeness. Given that I didn't have a three-dimensional model it was tricky; a lot had to come from my imagination."

"Yes, I can see how that would be difficult." Under the table, she clenched her hands not at all sure where this was going.

"When it was done, I wasn't happy with it. Something was missing but I never knew what. It was too..." He waved his hands as if searching for words. "Flat. The emotion in the painting was missing from the carving." He pushed his chair back and stood. "But yesterday, after you left, I felt inspired and began working on it again. I'd like you to take a look and give me your opinion."

She swallowed hard and forced an interested look onto her face. "I don't know if my opinion would be worth anything, but if it's anywhere near as good as your animal carvings, I'd like to see it."

Following Ben to the room where he worked on his hobby, she kept thinking of how to nonchalantly explain the resemblance, if his sculpture was, indeed, a good likeness to the painting. Maybe it wouldn't be obvious. After all, turning a painting into a sculpture was difficult; Ben had admitted as much.

But when he pulled the cloth covering off the piece, she gasped. It was her. She felt as if she was looking in a mirror. Yes, the reflection was made of wood, but it was so lifelike and...beautiful. Tears welled in her eyes and she had to give a small cough to clear her throat of the lump that seemed to have taken up residence.

"Ben, it's…it's amazing."

"Do you see it, Eugenie? It's you. Last night, when I finished, I thought perhaps I was imagining it but seeing you here standing beside it, there can be no mistake."

This was exactly what she'd been dreading. She wet her lips, preparing to explain but Ben continued talking.

"I was trying to figure out how this could be, but then I remembered you said you were originally from England. Could the woman in the painting be a relative?"

"Yes, that makes sense." She grasped onto his explanation like a lifeline. "Maybe a distant aunt or grandparent from generations back. Life is full of curious coincidences, isn't it?"

Ben nodded, turning the carving and glancing between it and her. "Yes, and I'm really glad this one happened or this sculpture would never have been completed. I can't believe I didn't see the resemblance earlier."

"People see what they want or expect to see."

"True." He stroked one finger along the cheek of the sculpture. "I must admit to being pleased with how well this turned out. You really inspired me."

She nodded. It *was* good and that gave her an idea. "Have you thought of trying to get an art gallery or dealer interested in your work? You might be able to sell this and your other carvings for a nice amount."

"Nah, my stuff isn't good enough. Well, maybe this is." He gestured at the carving. "But I don't think I'd ever want to sell it. It's sort of personal." He gave an awkward shrug. "As for the rest, they're just toys."

"But the figurines – the animals and birds – they're beautiful, so lifelike." She picked one up and turned it over in her hand, once again noting the attention to detail. "I almost expect it to start to move."

"It's all in the placement of limbs and the angle of the head." He reached out and touched the piece. "And here, the curve of the tail and the feathers."

His fingers brushed hers and she froze as tingles of awareness shot through her. He was so close, it muddled her thinking. Did he feel it too? She glanced up and found him looking at her, faint frown lines showing between his brows. Their gazes locked for one beat, then another and then, as one they both looked away.

Ben cleared his throat.

She blinked and forced herself to concentrate. This was a job, she was here to help Ben get his life straightened out. She looked down at the carving again.

"Well it's lovely and worthy of recognition."

He gave a smile. "When I was in college I used to dream of having an art show, but life didn't work out that way."

"You know, I noticed a little place close to my apartment, I think it was called the Maple Leaf Gallery. It's small but perhaps they might be interested in your work. And, if they aren't, they might know of someone who would be." She put down the carving, turned to him and smiled. "Please, let me try. What do you have to lose? The worst that can happen is they'll say no."

As if to reinforce her argument, the lights flickered and then went out.

"What happened?" She blinked in the gloom.

Ben scowled. "Either the blizzard has taken out the power or the electricity company has turned off my service."

"Are things really that bad?"

"Yeah," he sighed heavily, "they're really that bad."

"Well, then you have no choice but to try to sell some
of your work. It could prove to be the very source of income you need."

Ben agreed, albeit reluctantly and then mumbled about getting candles, a flashlight and starting a fire. Eugenie followed him out of the room while making mental notes on all she'd need to do in order for him to have a proper art show. She didn't know much about the topic but she was sure the new tablet with its almost magical internet would be able to help her.

She settled in the living room, her thoughts racing, barely registering Ben hunkering down by the fireplace and setting out candles. When he spoke, she gave a start.

"We'll save the flashlight for during the night. Right now, candles and firelight will have to do." He sank down beside her, his weight causing the cushions to dip so she slid against him.

"Sorry." She tried to hitch herself away but Ben slung his arm around her shoulder pulling her closer.

"It's okay. Its going to get cold in here tonight. Sharing body heat might be the best way to stay warm."

She nodded but found she was holding herself stiff despite the way the warmth of his body burned into her, threatening to melt her insides. Apart from when she'd rescued him in the snow, she'd never been this close to a man before. That time he'd been unconscious. Now, he was very much awake and she had to fight to stay composed.

The crackling of the fire was the only sound, Ben seeming content to stare at the burning logs, lost in his own thoughts, most likely his financial woes. Eugenie clasped her hands in her lap and watched the shadows cast on the wall by the candles that sat on the tables. To some it might have been romantic, but she had very little experience in that area and it mostly felt uncomfortable. Casual conversation or at least a distraction seemed to be called for.

"Ben, do you have any parlour games? Tiddlywinks or—"

"Parlour games?" He slid his gaze towards her and chuckled.

Darn. Obviously, her terminology was too antiquated – again. She really should have kept more up-to-date. "I mean cards or...er...I'm quite good at making shadow images..." She stuttered to a halt having no idea of the names of any current amusements. And shadow images? She'd done that with her nanny as a child. Why had she brought that up now? Awkward, awkward, awkward.

"Do you like marshmallows?"

Ben's question saved her from further fumbling and she grabbed on to it like a lifeline. "Would you believe I really don't know? I've heard of them, of course, but I've never had the opportunity to eat one. My parents were very strict." She had, indeed, heard of marshmallows. When she was alive they were a real treat and as such not something her parents considered necessary. She'd often wondered what they tasted like.

"Well it's time you were introduced." Ben disappeared into the kitchen. She could hear him rummaging about and then he reappeared with two wire coat hangers and a bag of what she assumed were marshmallows.

"You open the bag and I'll make us some skewers." He began to bend the metal back and forth until it broke in half and then he straightened it. "Here you go. Just stick the marshmallow on the end then hold it over the fire."

"Okay." She took one of the soft, squishy cylinders from the bag and poked it on the end of the stick as Ben instructed. As for putting it over the fire, she frowned.

"Like this." He slid off the couch and sat on the floor near the fire. "Hold one end of the wire while the end with the marshmallow is suspended over the flames."

She sat on the floor beside him and mimicked his actions, slowly twirling the stick. The marshmallow began to turn a golden brown.

"The trick is to get it brown on the outside but not black and don't let it catch fire." He reached out and pulled her hand back just as her marshmallow caught fire.

"Oops!"

He laughed and blew on it. "I'll eat it. I don't mind a bit of charcoal. You can have mine." He handed over his stick. "Don't pop it in your mouth right away or you'll get burnt. Blow on it a bit and then give it a test for temperature."

Once again, she followed his instructions and, deeming the marshmallow not too hot, took a bite.

"Mmm." The crispy outside contained a pool of melted sugary goo.

"So, what do you think?"

"It's good. Sweet and..." she licked her lips, "sticky."

"Yep. Want to try another one?"

"Sure."

They spent the next while toasting marshmallows. Ben offered her all sorts of silly bits of advice on the perfect toasting techniques and she laughed at his off-beat sense of humour. Eventually, despite his rather dubious help, she felt she was somewhat of an expert at the art.

"That was fun."

"It was." His eyes were twinkling, the edge of worry seeming to have disappeared.

"But I think I'm full." She smiled over at him.

"Me, too.   I'll put these back in the kitchen."   He moved to stand up but she caught his arm.

"Wait, you have a bit of marshmallow on you."   She reached out and unthinkingly brushed at a spot beside his mouth with her thumb, accidentally skimming his lips.

"Eugenie..." His eyes immediately darkened.

She froze, her hand still on his face.

He reached up, touched her hand, pressed a kiss to her palm.   The sensation shot up her arm and then down to her core.   Her breathing hitched and she really wasn't sure what she was feeling other than very confused.

"Ben..." Her mouth felt dry and she poked out the tip of her tongue to wet her lips.

Ben's gaze followed the action and then he leaned closer.   The air between them grew inexplicably charged and she found herself leaning closer, wanting to again experience the feel of his mouth on hers.   When it finally happened, she gasped.   His lips were warm, gentle, brushing hers, barely touching before pulling back.

He looked her in the eye.   "May I?"

She nodded and he kissed her again, this time more forcefully, exploring, tasting.   His tongue traced the seam of her lips and she found herself opening to him.   His hand cupped her cheek, then slid to cradle the back of her head. Somehow, she was on her back and he was leaning over her, the heat of his body and the nearby fire consuming her.   She traced her hands over his biceps and up to his broad shoulders, marvelling at the feel of him.

His hand was sliding down her body, cupping her breast.   Even through the material of her clothes she could feel the warmth, the brush of this thumb over her nipple. She arched her back pushing into his hand, wanting more of the amazing sensation.   This was wonderful, incredible.   She wanted, needed...

"Eugenie..." Ben pulled back.   His breathing was harsh.

She tugged at him, trying to draw him close again, kissing his jaw.

"We shouldn't. You barely know me." He shook his head.

"Ben..."

He was sitting up. "I didn't mean to do that." He scrubbed his hand over his face.

She mourned the loss of his warmth and weight but the distance was clearing her head, his words finally sinking into her brain. What had he said? He didn't mean... Oh no. Was this like her encounter with Jonathan? Was she reading more into the kisses than was really there?

"It's okay." She sat up and brushed her hair from her face. "I know a kiss doesn't really mean anything."

He stared at her for a moment before slowly nodding. "Right. It didn't mean anything."

She sensed a distinct lack of conviction in his words though.

Chapter 10

Ben squinted, wondering why the sun was shining in his eyes. He must have forgotten to draw the blinds before going to bed. Yawning, he began to do his usual morning stretch only to realize two things. There was a woman sleeping on his chest and he wasn't in his bed.

A glance down reminded him the woman was Eugenie. They'd ended up spending the night in the living room by the fire since it was the warmest room in the house. Sleeping bags and cushions had formed a makeshift mattress and he'd gathered blankets for them to snuggle under.

The impromptu sleeping arrangements had proven to be surprisingly comfortable. In fact, he couldn't recall when he'd slept better. Eugenie seemed to have that effect on him though. When she was around, the situation never seemed as bleak.

Without thinking, he pressed a kiss to the top of her head. She stirred against him and he held his breath, not wanting her to wake up. He was enjoying holding her, feeling her soft, womanly warmth sprawled on him, inhaling her scent with every breath. He'd never felt this way with his ex, not even in the early days. Truth be told, he'd been thinking with his crotch when he'd married Sabrina and, speaking of that part of his anatomy, it was reacting to Eugenie's presence.

He eased himself out from under her, leaving her sleeping while he wandered into the kitchen. The cold air was quickly solving the problem of the fit of his pants and he shivered as he found a match and lit the stove, thankful it was gas and not electric. At least he'd be able to make coffee.

"Ben?" Eugenie wandered into the kitchen just as the water began to boil.

"'Morning. I hope I didn't wake you.

"No. I needed to use the facilities." She rubbed her eyes and yawned widely. "It looks like the storm is over."

He glanced towards the window. "Yep. Once breakfast is done, I'll start shovelling the driveway. With any luck by the time I get to the road, a snow plow will have been by and I'll be able to get you home."

She moved to the cupboards and took out two mugs and set them on the table. "I'm in no rush."

"Well, that's a good thing because the driveway is pretty long. It will take a while to get it clear." He spooned instant coffee crystals into the mugs and then added the hot water. Eugenie, meanwhile, foraged in the fridge, taking out milk as well as eggs, butter and bread, shutting the door quickly to keep the cold in. There was a familiarity to how they seemed to work together. He smiled, liking the feeling of sharing his home with her.

As soon as breakfast was done he bundled up in heavy winter gear, grabbed a snow shovel and headed outside. Eugenie waved at him from the kitchen window. She'd volunteered to stay in and do the dishes, promising to come and help him as soon as she was done. He'd set out a toque, scarf and mitts, and left instructions for her to rummage through his room to find an extra sweatshirt as well as socks to wear over her own things since her coat and boots were more fashion than function.

He'd almost shovelled as far as the truck when he heard the backdoor open. Shielding his eyes against the glare of the sun off the snow he looked up to see Eugenie standing on the step. Her appearance had him giving a huff of laughter. Between the scarf and the toque, her head was almost completely covered, only her eyes peeking out.

"I'm ready to help!" Her words were muffled through the material as she began to climb down the steps, the extra clothing she was wearing making her movements awkward. Almost to the bottom, her foot somehow slipped and, arms flailing, she fell into a snowdrift.

"Eugenie? Are you okay?" He dropped his shovel and hurried over to find her on her back staring up at him.

She blinked, moved the scarf from over her mouth and gave a rueful smile. "Yes. Only my pride's injured."

He held out his hand and when she took it, he pulled her up. Having forgotten she was just a mite of a thing, he used more force than needed and she ended up pressed to his chest. It seemed the most natural thing in the world to hold her like that and dip his head down for a quick kiss. When he lifted his head, she looked up at him, eyes wide, the tip of her tongue sneaking out to taste her lips.

"Thank you." Her words came out barely above a whisper, the warmth of her breath feathering over his face in stark contrast to the cold winter air around them.

"No problem." He held her a moment longer before clearing his throat and letting her go.

"Do you have a spare shovel?"

"Yeah." He blinked trying to focus, fighting the urge to draw her into his arms again. "It's in the barn. You use this one. I'll go get the other." Handing her his shovel, he made his way to the barn, wading through the drifts while Chip frolicked about barking and diving into snowbanks. The crazy animal had always loved the snow.

He and Eugenie worked together to clear the driveway. Whenever they paused to rest, she'd marvel at the beauty of the snow, pointing out how it adorned the branches of the trees or the way it swirled around the base of the trunks. At one point, he found himself staring at her mitten-covered hand as she exclaimed over the intricacies of snowflakes. It was funny, how he hadn't noticed the beauty of the weather for years but an hour with Eugenie had him seeing everything with new eyes. Sort of like the carving he'd never been able to get right but once she appeared, his fingers knew exactly what to do.

"Ben, I need to take a break." Eugenie was leaning against her shovel, breathing hard.

"Yeah, me too. Let's head inside, have a snack and get warmed up." He propped his shovel against the side of the truck and started to walk back to the house when something suddenly hit him in the back of the head. "Hey!"

He turned to see Eugenie smiling mischievously and forming another snowball with her hands.

"Sorry." She shrugged. "I've never thrown a snowball before and didn't want to miss out on the opportunity."

"And you couldn't throw it at a tree?"

"A moving target seemed more challenging."

"You realize this calls for revenge?" He bent down to gather snow in his hand.

Her eyes widened as he took aim and lobbed a snowball at her. "Ben!"

He hadn't thrown the snow very hard but it still made a satisfying splat against her coat. She narrowed her eyes, tossed her own snowball and the war began. For the next few minutes they threw snowballs at each other, hiding behind trees and using the truck for shelter. Eventually, Eugenie began waving her snow-covered hat back and forth like a flag.

"I surrender. I surrender."

He trudged over and picked her up. She squealed and pushed at his shoulders.

"What are you doing?"

"The victor gets the spoils of war."

"I'm not a *spoil*, Ben."

"No, there's definitely nothing spoiled about you." He loosened his hold and she slid down the front of him. He studied her features, her sparkling eyes, the tendrils of hair that curled about her flushed cheeks, her beckoning lips. "*You* are perfection."

With that, he kissed her, walking her backwards until she was pressed against the truck. He leaned into her, letting her feel his weight as he ravaged her mouth. She responded to him so sweetly, at first tentative, unsure, then with growing boldness. Last night, he'd sensed her inexperience. It was the only reason he'd stopped. It had been ages since he'd been with a woman and his willpower had been sorely tested. Now, his need was getting the better of him. He pushed his leg between her thighs, moving against her. Somehow, he had his gloves off, his hands inside her coat, cupping her breasts as she clutched his back, soft sounds of encouragement coming from her throat.

"Eugenie, I—"

The blast of a horn had him suddenly pulling back. A snow plow was stopped at the end of his driveway, the operator climbing out of the cab.

"You folks okay?" The man called out cheerfully, either not knowing or caring what he'd just interrupted.

"Yeah, we're fine." Ben walked towards the man, trying to ignore the fact that his pants definitely felt tighter than they had a few minutes earlier.

"Power lines are down a few miles back so I've been checking on everyone just to be sure."

"We have a fireplace, so we survived."

"Good to know." The plow driver glanced the length of the driveway. "Looks like you have a lot of shovelling to do."

Ben glanced back at the distance that still had to be cleared and sighed. "A long driveway has its disadvantages."

The man rubbed his neck. "We're only supposed to do the county roads but I can clear this out for you. It will only take a few minutes, just don't tell my boss."

"That would be great. Thanks." Getting the driveway cleared was worth having that kiss interrupted. Well...he surreptitiously rearranged himself in his pants...almost.

Eugenie stood on the back step watching Ben talk to the snow plow driver. She tilted her head and squinted. The man looked very familiar.

Zeke?

She planted her hands on her hips, wondering what the GA was up to. His timing was horrible, interrupting the kiss she'd been sharing with Ben.

She licked her lips, still able to taste Ben. It was addictive and she wondered if all kisses were that way or if Ben's were a cut above the rest. Whatever the case, she knew she wanted to experience it again. And the feel of his body against hers. It had made her weak at the knees. In fact, she'd been thankful for the presence of the truck behind her or she might very well have collapsed in the snow.

Ben wasn't indifferent to her either. She might not know a lot about men but she knew enough about anatomy to be well aware of what that bulge in his pants meant. Even through her layers of clothing she'd been able to feel it and when he'd moved his hips against her, well, she'd responded in kind, her body seeming to have a mind of its own.

"The plow driver is going to clear the rest of the driveway for us." Ben called out as he approached.

"That's nice of him."

"And he says the power lines are down so I guess they didn't turn off my electricity. Apparently, I won't be condemned to living like a pioneer after all."

"Good." She glanced over Ben's shoulder in time to catch Zeke giving her a jaunty salute. Was he responsible for the electricity? Had Michael sent Zeke to help her or was it the GA's own idea? Inwardly, she frowned not sure she liked the idea of having someone checking up on her. Plus, he'd interrupted her kiss. Yes, she'd definitely have words with him the next time they met.

She followed Ben inside and then, after a short break for a warming cup of coffee, they went back out to brush the fresh snow from the truck. It didn't take long after that for them to be on their way into town.

High piles of snow lined the road and all along the way there were people digging out their driveways. A lucky few had snow blowers; noisy machines that almost chewed through the snow and spewed it out in a white powdery stream.

"I think you need to get one of those, Ben."

He made a face. "If I could afford one."

Right. She frowned, his finances once again filling her thoughts. After he dropped her off at her place, she'd search out the gallery she'd seen. With any luck, the owner would be willing to display a few of Ben's pieces. Artists didn't make much unless they were well-known, she knew that, but every little bit helped.

"Here we are." Ben pulled up to the curb and turned off the engine.

With a start, she realized they'd arrived at her apartment. The stately old building looked much finer bedecked with snow than it did the rest of the time, taking on an almost gingerbread house type of appearance with the snow being the frosting. The exterior stairs to her apartment had snow on each step and reminded her of a picture book illustration of clouds ascending to Heaven. How apropos!

"Well, thanks for the ride." She placed her hand on the door handle and glanced at Ben.

"No problem." He gave a nod, his gaze drifting over her face.

She hesitated not sure what the protocol was. They'd kissed three times now. Did he want to kiss her again? She hoped so. Maybe she should be bold and lean towards him? Just as she was about to do so, he cleared his throat.

"Eugenie."

"Yes?"

His hands flexed on the steering wheel and he half turned towards her.

Her breath caught in her throat, warmth flooding her in anticipation but then he gave his head a barely perceptible shake and eased back in his seat.

"I have some errands to run today so by the time I get back it will be too late to get any work done."

"Okay." Disappointed, she opened the door and cool air immediately filled the small space. "I'll see you tomorrow then?"

"Sure. If the buses aren't running, I can come and pick you up."

"Thanks." She hesitated, not wanting to leave but knowing she had to. It was obvious Ben had had enough of her company.

Just as she was going to exit the truck, he reached across and brushed the back of his knuckles over her cheek. "I enjoyed roasting marshmallows with you last night. I hope we can do it again sometime."

Shocked, she nodded and almost fell out of the truck.

Ben started the vehicle and through the windshield she could see him nodding toward the house. He wanted her to go inside before he left. The gentlemanly gesture had her smiling and she felt like she floated up the stairs, a warm bubble of happiness filling her. Ben cared for her, she was sure of it!

Chapter 11

Eugenie still felt as if she were floating on a cloud as she turned her key in the lock and entered her little apartment.

"Is that you under all those clothes, Eugenie?"

"Whaa…?" She spun around to face the overstuffed armchair in the corner of her living room. The TV was on some music station and Zeke was ensconced in her home. He'd made himself well and truly comfortable with a huge double-decker sandwich and a soft drink. She didn't know she'd had that much food in the kitchen!

Surprise quickly turned to anger. "Zeke! What are you doing here? What if I'd invited Ben up? How would I have explained the presence of the snow plow man in my living room eating my food and watching my television?"

"No need to get your halo bent out of shape, Babe. If I'd heard him coming up those stairs with you I'd have simply disappeared."

To demonstrate, both he and his meal vanished without even a whiff of the salami in his sandwich left behind. A second later the remote lifted and switched off the TV before settling back on the side table.

"Okay, very impressive. Now come back because you and I need to have words!" She unwrapped her scarf then pulled off her hat and mittens while she waited for him to reappear. Finally, he materialized back in the chair, his plate and drink in his hands. "Well? What have you got to say for yourself?"

"Umm… I got bored waiting for you and when I checked your fridge you had way too much food in there. I know you only keep it stocked to help maintain your cover so I thought I'd help you out. Can't have it spoiling, right?"

"You know perfectly well I'm not talking about you eating my food. Why were you driving that snow plow? Where's the human who should've been doing that job? And why are you spying on me? Did Michael send you?"

"Whoa! Too many questions. Let me see." He laid his food on the side table. "I've always wanted to drive one of those things. He stopped off at a café to have a hot breakfast. I'm not. And he didn't." Zeke checked off his answers against his fingers.

"If you're not spying on me, why are you here?"

"My other assignment is mostly night work and I'm at a loose end during the day so I thought I'd pop down to see if I could help out." Zeke had taken a huge bite of sandwich and Eugenie had to struggle not to tell him to stop speaking with food in his mouth.

Eugenie took off her coat and hung it up by the door. "Well, I *am* glad you're here, because I could do with some advice."

"As long as you keep food like this in your kitchen, I'm your man." He took another bite.

"Let me get a hot drink first; it's really cold out there and I'm still not able to cope with such low temperatures." She began to walk towards the kitchen when a steaming cup of coffee appeared on a table. Her gaze flicked from the cup to Zeke. "You're showing off!"

"Yep." He grinned unrepentantly.

Shaking her head, she picked up the mug and sat down on the couch. "Zeke, I'm not sure how to word this."

"Just open your mouth and allow the words to flow. That's usually the easiest way."

She almost snorted her coffee through her nose as she laughed at him. However, it put her at ease and she decided to go ahead and ask.

"Have you ever kissed a human, Zeke?"

Zeke spluttered as he, too, almost choked on his drink. "Now, that's a loaded question, Eugenie. Why do you want to know?"

"Because I've kissed Ben. Or rather, he's kissed me. Three times. You interrupted the last one." She slid a scowl his way at the memory.

"Sorry about that. I guess I need to work on my timing." He shrugged. "Anyway, did you like it? The kiss, I mean, not the interruption."

She gave him a frustrated look. "You're not answering my question. I asked if *you* have ever kissed a human, not me. And what about sex? Have you had sex with a human?"

"Okay, okay, yes I've kissed a human. Yes, I liked it, but then it's no different from kissing a fellow angel so no surprise there. As to sex. No, not with a human. Although, I wouldn't say no. I'm guessing there's not the same *connection* you get when making love with a fellow angel but I'm betting it's just as good."

Eugenie sighed and stared down at her feet. "I don't know what to do, Zeke."

"Tell me this, Babe. Does Michael know you're playing tonsil hockey with your client?"

She looked up at his words. "Tonsil hockey? Is that some kind of modern slang?"

"Nah, it's been around for ages. Well? Does he?"

"Yes."

"And did you get a reprimand?"

"No."

"Then you don't have a problem. Do whatever comes naturally, and more importantly, enjoy yourself."

"But… I'm a… I've never…" She could feel her face heating up. She knew Zeke was looking at her but she refused to meet his gaze.

"What? You've never?" Zeke's eyebrows shot upwards. "Not even when you were alive?"

Eugenie shook her head, feeling miserable.

Zeke put his plate down and stood up to walk over to the couch. After sitting down next to her, he put his arm around her shoulders and hugged her gently to his side. "Oh Babe. If it feels right with Ben then let it happen. He seems like a nice guy and he'll be good for you. You'll understand his psyche better for being intimate."

He put his hand over hers on her mug of coffee. "Drink up. Is there anything else I can help you with?"

She sipped at her drink and thought about Ben and his financial worries. Earlier she'd considered going to the gallery she'd seen in the hope they might want to display his carvings. But they wouldn't agree to show anything sight unseen. She explained this to Zeke, whom she was fast coming to think of as a brother and friend.

"That's one problem that's easily solved. Just pop back to Ben's place with your tablet, remain invisible, take some pictures then pop back here and trot off to the gallery." His cheeky grin made her smile, making her feel so much better than she had a few minutes earlier. Then she remembered something and put down her mug.

"I've not mastered that being invisible and handling tangible things trick. What you did earlier, picking up the remote control while invisible and turning the television off, I've not learned to do that yet.

"No problem, Babe. I'll let you in on a secret, not a lot of GAs can do the hovering between worlds trick. I've been working on it and you're the only person who knows I can do it now. Once you get a few more centuries under your belt, you'll be an expert. But for now, tell me what to take pics of and I'll go do it for you."

"Thank you, Zeke!" She hugged him, thinking what an amazing friend he was. "I'd be totally lost on this assignment without your help."

Zeke laughed and stood up, brushing crumbs from his jeans. "Glad to be of help. I'll get this little job done and then I'd better be on my way. Believe it or not I do have an assignment of my own, even though it's not taking up my time night and day.

Sometime later, Eugenie paused outside the Maple Leaf Gallery she'd seen earlier in the week. The window displayed several paintings and sculptures, some still life and others more abstract. She cocked her head trying to determine what one of them might be depicting but soon gave up. Ben's work was much more to her taste.

A woman was working on the displays, adding bits of fluffy cotton that looked like snow and some sprigs of holly. When she noticed Eugenie's interest, she smiled and nodded towards the entrance. Taking a deep breath, Eugenie pushed open the door hoping she'd be able to convince the woman to accept some of Ben's work.

As soon as she entered the gallery, she noticed the subtle scent of wood and paint. Soft music played in the background and spotlighting was carefully arranged to showcase each artistic piece to the best advantage.

"Hello." The woman from the window greeted her. "I saw you looking at some of the pieces in the window. Are you interested in anything particular?"

Eugenie immediately noticed the woman was tall and perfectly coiffed with flawless makeup and long manicured nails. In comparison, she knew she probably looked a fright, her hair blown about by the wind. She was wearing Ben's scarf, too, and it had definitely seen better days. But, she wasn't here to impress the woman with her appearance. She was here to help Ben and so she pushed her own insecurities to the side. "Actually, I was wondering how an artist manages to get their work displayed here?"

The woman's smile faltered. "I'm sorry but we have quite high standards as you can see." She gestured about the room. "We don't accept just anyone who stops in, though I'm sure your work is delightful in a primitive sort of way."

Eugenie was sure she'd been insulted but pinned a smile on her face anyway. "It's not my work, it's my friend's. He does amazing life-like carvings."

"Well, I'd have to see a sample, naturally." The woman sniffed.

"I have pictures," Eugenie pulled her tablet out of her purse and flipped to the images Zeke had taken. "See?"

The woman glanced down and then did a double take. "Those are good." She took the tablet from Eugenie's hand and flipped through the images. "Very good."

"He's a local artist and he's never displayed his work before. It's mostly a hobby but—"

"This is exactly what I'm looking for." The woman walked over to an elegant table set to one side and picked up a leaflet. "We're trying something new this year for the holidays; having a show that features local artists. It's very exclusive and we thoroughly vet the work to ensure it meets the standards our patrons have come to expect. From the look of these images, your friend certainly fits the bill."

"I'm sure he does." Eugenie nodded eagerly.

"Show him this leaflet and, if he's interested, have him bring in a few pieces so I can see his actual work. Photos can be deceiving, as I'm sure you're well aware."

Eugenie felt her temper rise. The woman had implied the images of Ben's work had been doctored. Reining in her ire, she agreed. "I'll have him stop by sometime during the next few days."

"Excellent. Have him ask for me, Daphne Standish."

"I will."

As she left the gallery, Eugenie was torn between excitement for Ben and strange sense of impending doom. There was something about Daphne Standish that set her teeth on edge.

Chapter 12

The next morning Ben was working in his shop when the door opened letting in a rush of cold air as well as a swirl of snow.

"Hello, Ben. Hello, Chip."

Chip gave a low woof and thumped the floor with his tail as Eugenie entered the barn.

"'Morning Eugenie." Ben smiled at the woman who entered his makeshift workshop. Flakes of snow clung to the strands of hair that poked out from under the toque she wore. Some women might fuss about their appearance but he thought her dishevelled look was adorable and real.

"It's certainly cold today."

"Winter in Canada." He watched as she shivered and brushed snow from her coat. "You mustn't have lived here long."

"Er...no. I travelled quite a bit after leaving England. Spent some time in warmer countries." She pulled the hat from her head and handed it to him. "Here. Thanks for letting me borrow it."

"Keep it. I have others."

"Thanks." She grinned at him. "I'm impressed with how quickly the roads were cleared and the buses running again."

"We're used to cleaning up after a big snowstorm."

"Did you get your errands done yesterday?" She pulled off her gloves and took off her coat.

"Yeah." He sighed heavily. "I managed to get an extension on some of the bills but I think I'm fighting a losing battle. Even with the furniture sales you managed to arrange, it will only be a short time before the bank forecloses." He bent over the piece of wood he was sanding, not wanting her to see the despair he was feeling. Her opinion mattered to him. It was one of the reasons he didn't have a hangover this morning. In the past, he'd 'celebrated' bad news by drinking himself into a stupor but last night, knowing he'd be seeing Eugenie in a few hours, he'd taken his frustration out on chopping wood for the fireplace.

"But I have good news! A local art gallery has all but agreed to display your carvings in a show."

"Really?" He slowly straightened.

"Yes. Naturally you have to bring in a few pieces to be assessed first, but that's normal procedure. I'm sure they'll accept your work."

He rubbed the back of his neck, not sure how he felt. It would be exciting to see his work in a show; it had been a dream of his years ago, but what were the chances the gallery owner would agree to include them? Was he up for more rejection? "I don't know, Eugenie."

"Ben, this could be your big break. People will see your work and love it and buy it and—"

Her enthusiasm made him smile. "Slow down there. Even if the gallery agrees—and that's a big *if*—chances are I won't sell anything. Maybe a piece or two at best. Hardly enough—"

She stepped forward and pressed her hand to his chest. "Ben, you have to try. You have to have faith. Please?"

He looked down at her face, so earnest, so full of life and hope. "Okay, for you, Eugenie. I'll give it a try."

She positively beamed at his words and raised up on her toes to press a quick kiss to his lips. "Thank you. I know you won't be sorry. Right after lunch I'll help you pick out a few carvings and we'll take them into town."

He nodded feeling a bit as if he was being steamrolled. Eugenie might appear to be a quiet little thing, but she had a strength of will he was only now starting to see.

Later that day, they drove into town and pulled up in front of a gallery. He'd vaguely noticed it before but it was one of those classy-looking establishments he'd never even consider entering. His ex had loved to shop at places like that though and it was the bills she'd brought home along with dubious works of art that had totally turned him off.

"Come on, Ben." Eugenie stood on the sidewalk waiting for him and he realized he'd been staring at the building, gripping the steering wheel tightly, caught up in the past.

He climbed out of the truck and picked up the box containing the carvings they'd decided to show the gallery owner. Eugenie had wanted him to bring along the bust but he'd refused. It was personal and it reminded him so much of her, he'd never want to part with it. Someday, when she'd moved on, he'd still have the carving to look at and remember her by.

The door of the gallery chimed softly as they entered and Ben felt his throat tighten as he looked around. What was he doing in a place like this? With his work boots and old jeans, he felt like a country bumpkin. Eugenie, however, seemed to have no compunction about approaching an attendant and asking to see the owner.

"Daphne Standish, please. She asked us to stop by."

"Indeed?" The attendant looked them up and down then disappeared into a back room. A few minutes later, he returned with a tall blonde woman.

"Hello, Mrs. Standish. We spoke yesterday. I brought along the artist I was telling you about and some samples of his work."

The woman flicked her glance over Eugenie and then looked at him. A smile slowly spread over her unnaturally red lips. "Well, hello. I'm Daphne Standish. I'm pleased to meet you...?"

"Ben. Ben Davis." Ben stuck out his hand and shook hers, noting her nails were long and the same red as her lips. "Mrs. Standish."

"It's Ms. But please, call me Daphne."

He nodded and, feeling uncomfortable with the almost feral gleam in Ms. Standish's eyes as she looked him up and down, he shifted the box he held under one arm. "Eugenie said you'd like to see some of my work?"

"Yes. We're a very exclusive gallery and don't carry the work of just anyone who calls themselves an artist."

She indicated a table at the side and Ben set the box there. Eugenie took off the lid and withdrew one of the pieces, handing it to Daphne.

"Hmm..." Daphne turned the piece in her hand, running her fingers over the wood, turning it at various angles. "This is quite good. May I see what else you have?"

They took the other samples out and with each new piece, Daphne's smile grew. In the end, her enthusiasm was contagious and Ben felt his trepidation melting away. The woman genuinely thought his work was good. Before he quite knew what was happening he was agreeing for her to stop by his house to pick out the pieces she thought would work best for the show and he had a sales contract in his hand.

After they left the gallery and were back in the truck, he was still bemused at what had just happened.

"Isn't this exciting?" Eugenie reached over and hugged his arm. "I'm so happy for you, Ben."

"Thanks." He folded the contract and stuck it in his pocket. "I'll read this over tonight before I sign it."

"Good idea but I'm sure it's standard."

"Probably, however, after my business partner screwed me over, I'm a lot less trusting than I used to be." He started the truck and headed towards Eugenie's place.

"I think I know a lawyer who could read it over for you if you want."

"An honest one?"

"Definitely. He'd have to be honest to live... I mean, work where he does. The...company...is very particular about who they let in."

That night Eugenie went to see Michael, Ben's contract with the gallery in her hand. She was sure there were several lawyers in Heaven she could ask to peruse the contact, she just wanted to ask Michael which one to approach.

She'd called ahead this time, not wanting to repeat the mistake of her previous visit. Michael was a busy man—even more so than she'd initially thought—and she didn't want to disturb him. Her tentative tap on the door was immediately answered and Michael, smartly dressed in a suit and tie, stood up and walked towards her as she entered.

"Eugenie, prompt as always. What can I do for you?" He gestured to a seat and she sat down while he circled to his side of the desk.

"I was wondering if you could recommend a good lawyer?"

"A lawyer?" He raised a brow and smiled, leaning back in his chair. "You've broken the law?"

"No! At least I don't think I have. I..." She paused and considered her conduct of late and then shook her head. "No. I'm sure I haven't. This is for Ben. He has to sign a contract with an art gallery and, because his previous business partner screwed him, he wants to make sure there's nothing untoward about it."

"*Screwed him?*" The corner of Michael's mouth twitched. There was a definite air of amusement about him.

"I believe that's the term he used, sir." She frowned. "Or maybe it was *screwed him over?*"

"I think that might be the phrase you wanted." Michael chuckled and held out his hand. "May I see this contract?"

"Of course." She slid it across the desk and watched as Michael scanned the piece of paper.

"It seems standard but I'll have our legal team look it over and get right back to you." With a negligent wave of his hand the contract disappeared.

"Thank you, sir. I really appreciate this. I wouldn't want Ben to end up being taken advantage of because of my idea."

"And what idea is that?"

She explained about the gallery and concluded with a nod. "I think the case might be almost over. If Ben is discovered at the art show, and I'm sure he will be because he's very talented, well then he'll become rich and famous and his troubles will be over." She folded her hands in her lap and smiled, though a part of her wasn't completely pleased the assignment would soon be over.

Michael gave her an enigmatic look. "You need to be careful, Eugenie. Never bet on the future because the path you see set out before you can, in the blink of an eye, disappear in the mist. It all rests on Ben's decisions."

"He'll make the right choice. I know he was hesitant at first about the gallery show but I can see his faith in himself growing."

"Faith in oneself is very important." Michael nodded. "However, what about his faith in people, in relationships? Is that growing too? Benjamin has been deeply hurt, those he trusted turned on him. Humans need to know they can depend on others. Living in isolation isn't good for them."

She frowned. "He's mentioned his business partner. As I said, that's why he wanted the contract read over."

"That's just good business sense. I'm wondering if Benjamin is opening up to you. It's important for him to have people in his life. He wasn't meant to live as a hermit. And the same goes for you. Your experience in life was limited. Are you willing to take risks?"

She nodded but then thought about Jonathan and how hurt she'd been when she'd discovered he was married. Of course, that had been years ago, and it had been a really brief encounter. In fact, she'd often wondered in the intervening years if it had been wishful thinking on her part. It wasn't still affecting her today, was it?

A movement caught her attention. The contract had reappeared on Michael's desk. After glancing at a sticky note attached to it, he peeled the message off and passed the contract to her. "It's perfectly safe for Ben to sign this."

"Thank you, sir. And, please, thank the legal team for me as well." She rose to her feet, preparing to leave.

"You're very welcome, Eugenie. But remember what I said. Being open to new relationships is important. A guardian angel has to be able to relate to a wide variety of persons."

"Yes, I'll keep that in mind, sir."

A wide variety of persons. She mulled that over as she headed back to her apartment. But did she want a wide variety, or…did she just want Ben?

Chapter 13

Over the next few weeks, Ben switched his focus from furniture to his carvings and bowls, preparing more pieces for the art show. Daphne had been to the farm several times to look at his work, trying to pick the carvings that best showcased his skill. It was nerve-wracking, having someone examine his work so critically. Chip didn't seem to like it either, growling each time the woman stopped by. Her silver sports car seemed incongruous parked in front of his place as did her heels and designer clothing as she walked through his tired house. Not that it mattered; she was there for his art work, not the state of his home.

The carving of Eugenie, as he now called it, had especially captured the woman's attention.

"Benjamin, you really need to include this." Lips pursed, she'd examined the carving with a critical eye.

"No. I don't want to sell it."

"It doesn't have to have a price tag. It could be the centrepiece of the show. Think of the attention it would garner."

"It might but I don't want to share it." He'd placed a cloth over the bust and drawn her attention to another item.

Daphne had let the matter drop that day but he could tell she hadn't given up on convincing him.

Beyond Daphne's visits, life continued much as it had before. Eugenie arrived each day and worked on sorting the collectibles in the barn. He'd use his lathe to form bowls or he'd bring a carving out so he could work and keep her company. She protested he didn't need to be there but he enjoyed their conversations. Besides, the house was lonely when she wasn't in it.

He considered that point. When had that changed? It seemed only a few weeks ago he'd been enjoying his own company. Now he found himself looking out the window every morning, anticipating Eugenie's arrival and, at the end of the day, he was reluctant to let her go. They'd share supper and then sit by the fire talking and roasting marshmallows for dessert. She'd even shown him her mastery of shadow puppets.

He chuckled at the memory of how that night had ended, a playful kiss on her hand had evolved into him kissing a variety of other body parts too. As always though, he'd stopped when things were getting too hot and heavy. Eugenie wasn't the type of woman one had a casual sexual encounter with. No, sex with her would mean something and was he ready to risk that again? He wasn't sure.

Eyes narrowed, he studied her as she worked. She was nibbling on her lip, flicking her gaze between an old lantern she held in her hand and something on her tablet. The pile of what he'd considered junk was shrinking. What would happen when she was finally done? The idea of not seeing her again was like a cold weight in his stomach. Without thinking, he stood up and walked over to her.

"Eugenie?"

She looked up from her work at the sound of Ben's voice. As usual his clothes were festooned with wood shavings and his thick brown hair wasn't quite as dark as it should be due to the sawdust that had drifted on to it.

"Yes, Ben?"

"What do you have there?" He nodded towards the item in her hand.

"A finger kerosene lamp. I found it packed in an old crate."

"Finger?"

"Yes. See the glass loop on the base where you'd hook your finger?"

He nodded. "Is it worth much?"

"Not a great deal from what I can tell. Maybe twenty dollars. The chimney has a chip but its still pretty to look at and the detail in the cut-glass base is gorgeous when the light shines through it." She turned it in her hand before carefully setting it back in the crate.

"You're making good progress." He glanced along the back of the barn. There's so much stuff gone that I can actually see the wall."

She nodded. "You'll have a lot more room to work. Maybe you can even create a proper display area for your furniture."

"Good idea." He slung one arm around her shoulder and kissed her temple.

The simple gesture filled her with a warm, happy feeling. They were so comfortable around each other. It was hard to believe there had ever been a time when she hadn't known him. She loved spending time with him and hated to see each day end. When he took her home in the evenings, he'd press a lingering kiss to her lips before pulling away with obvious reluctance. At night, she hugged her pillow and wished he was beside her. Some days she didn't even remember she was here on an assignment!

And that reminded her... She moved to look up at him. "I have good news for you!"

"And what might that be?"

"I sold several of the collectibles. I set up an account online and posted pictures of them. I just have to ship them to the buyer."

"Fantastic. I can drive you to the post office."

"Do you want to know how much your percentage of the sale price works out to?" The amount she quoted him had his eyes widening. She left out the small detail that she'd fudged her records so he was getting one hundred percent of the profits. After all, she had no need of money in Heaven.

"I'm surprised you could get that much for what I thought was junk."

"It's not a fortune but every bit helps, right?" She smiled, pleased with her efforts.

Chip chose that moment to nose his way between them, managing to sit on Ben's feet while leaning against Eugenie's legs, effectively claiming both of them. They'd laughed and given him several pats before getting back to work.

Ben helped her package the items she'd sold and ready them for shipping. She'd already neatly printed out labels at her apartment last night, now all they needed was postage. "I'll take them to the post office for you tomorrow." Ben offered. He was holding her hand as they walked to the house for dinner. Of late, he seemed to assume she'd stay to share a meal with him. It was yet another little thing that filled her with happiness.

The fact Ben's art show was the next day dominated dinner conversation and carried over to their time in front of the fire. Ben expressed his inner doubts and she did her best to alleviate them.

"Your carvings are wonderful. Everyone will love them."

"I think you're biased."

She was tucked up against his side, sitting on the floor, their backs against the sofa. Her head was resting on his shoulder and she tipped her head up to look at him. "Maybe, but I also know amazing when I see it." She stretched a bit and kissed him.

When she would have pulled away, he cupped the back of her head and drew her closer for another kiss. "I know amazing when I see it, too." His gaze travelled over her face and she felt her face heat under his intense scrutiny.

"I'm not amazing."

His thumb stroked her cheek. "And that's why you are."

"I don't understand."

"You don't realize how wonderful you are. It's not some act where you pretend to be modest to get another compliment. You're genuine."

"Well, thank you." She wasn't sure how to respond.

"You've taken time out of your own life to help me; sorting and selling the stuff in the barn, arranging the art show, dragging in customers to buy my furniture."

"I didn't exactly drag them in."

"You know what I mean." He shook his head. "You even inspired me to finish that sculpture of the artist's model."

"I—"

"Thank you, Eugenie, for coming into my life." He kissed her slowly, tenderly.

She responded in kind, reaching up to touch his face, then stroke his hair.

Eventually, he bore her backward until she was lying on the carpet, his body pressed to hers. She caressed his shoulders, not for the first time, marvelling at their breadth, then traced her way down the indent of his spine and back up again.

His hand was on her breast, stroking and kneading as their kisses became more intense. Warmth began to bloom down low in her abdomen and she found her hips were moving against his of their own volition.

"Eugenie," he pulled away, breathing heavily. "I think—"

"Don't stop, Ben. Please." She grasped his head and kissed him again. "I love you. I want to be with you."

"You what?"

"I'm sorry. I shouldn't have said that." She couldn't believe she'd actually spoke the words that had been burning in her heart and turned her head away in shame.

He took her chin in his hand and forced her to meet his gaze. "Don't be embarrassed. I...I love you, too."

"You do? Oh Ben, I can't believe it!" She wrapped her arms around him and he laughed softly.

"Why so surprised? What is there about you not to love?" He gazed down at her. "You have beautiful eyes, amazing cheek bones, plump lips..." He pressed a kiss to each feature as he spoke. "A long slender neck and this little area here..." He pushed the top of her blouse open and brushed his lips over the hollow at the base of her throat, "intrigues me."

He continued on, moving lower, leaving little open-mouthed kisses on the exposed skin as he unbuttoned her shirt and brushed her bra aside. When he finally kissed her breast, her back arched and she gave a cry of delight.

"You like that?" He grinned.

"Yes." She breathed out on a sigh.

"Then you're going to love what comes next." He took her nipple in his mouth and sucked gently. She was sure her eyes were rolling back in her head.

She tugged at his shirt, freeing it from his jeans and slipping her hands underneath, eager to give him equal pleasure. From the sound that came from his throat, he seemed to like her efforts.

Stroking, kissing, the sound of zippers being undone and rustling material filled the room, joining with the crackling of the fire as they explored each other. Somehow, she still had presence of mind to make sure a targeted mind wipe was in place so her wing flaps wouldn't register on his consciousness.

"Are you sure, Eugenie?" He loomed over her, the firelight highlighting his sculpted muscles.

"Yes, except...I've never done this." She tensed, not sure how he'd receive the news.

He pulled back. "You're a virgin?"

She nodded. "Does it matter? I'll try to make it good for you."

"Oh, sweetheart." He shook his head and kissed her tenderly. "That's supposed to be my line."

"It is?"

"Your first time should be special and I'm honoured you want it to be with me."

She relaxed as she saw the look of love in his eyes, the caring, the tenderness.

"I'll go get some protection." He began to rise.

"No. I...er...I'm protected." She quickly improvised knowing she couldn't get pregnant and not wanting him to leave.

"Are you sure?" At her nod he settled over her again then resumed kissing her until she was lost in a sea of sensation. There was a hard, probing warmth, a feeling of pressure followed by a slight pain and a feeling of fullness and then...then the most amazing experience of all.

She clutched Ben tightly, arms and legs wrapped around his solid body as he took her on a journey to a plane she'd never known existed, one filled with pleasure almost too great to bear, one that had her muscles tightening, her body arching as she hovered on the edge until she lost control and all sensation exploded in pulsing ecstasy.

Afterwards, he held her close, whispering gently as she drifted off to sleep feeling warm and secure and loved in a way she'd never thought possible.

Ben woke the next morning with a smile on his face. That hadn't happened in ages, but he knew why today was different. After Eugenie had fallen asleep in his arms he'd carried her to bed and now she was snuggled against his side.

He turned his head so he could see her. She was sleeping soundly, her lashes fanned out over her cheeks, her breath tickling his chest. So beautiful. It seemed too good to be true that she'd appeared in his life. What had he done to deserve her?

It was with reluctance that he looked at the alarm clock and realized he had to get up. He needed to get Eugenie's packages to the post office and he hoped to finish one more piece for the art show tonight.

He kissed her awake which turned into far more than just kisses. As a result, it was some time before, satiated, they finally made it out of bed.

"You can use the shower first while I make breakfast." He pulled on his jeans and stretched.

"You could join me." She looked up shyly at him through her lashes and he laughed.

"If I do that we'll never get anything done today. Now scoot." He took her by the shoulders and turned her towards the bathroom then gave her a gentle push.

"Spoilsport." She stuck her tongue out playfully before hurrying from the room.

Grinning, he headed to the kitchen and began to get out eggs and milk and bread. The sun streamed through the window, filling the room with brightness and pushing away the early morning chill. Just like Eugenie, he mused. She was his own beam of sunshine.

After breakfast, he loaded the packages of collectibles onto his truck in preparation for going to the post office. Eugenie planned on staying behind to do a bit more sorting.

"I want to finish that one box first," she explained as he climbed into the truck. "Then I'm heading home to get ready for your big night."

"Yeah," he sighed, doubt filling him again. "I still wonder if this was a good idea. My work is—"

She pressed a finger to his lips. "Your work is wonderful. You just don't want to get dressed up in a suit and tie tonight."

"Well, there is that." He made a face thinking of all the stuffy affairs he'd had to go to with his ex.

"You'll look handsome. They'll love your work. Now, go!"

Chapter 14

Eugenie watched Ben drive away, her brow wrinkled thoughtfully. He really needed this show. Not only financially but to boost his self-confidence. Hearing people, complete strangers, exclaim over his work, would be good for him.

Nodding her head, she went back inside, wanting to tidy the kitchen before starting to work in the barn. Sorting through the boxes and piles was almost like hunting for treasure and quite addictive. She'd just started the dishes when Chip started barking which could only mean one thing. Ms. Standish. Darn.

The woman made her feel uncomfortable though she wasn't exactly sure why. Sighing to herself, she greeted her at the door with, hopefully, a genuine smile on her face. "Good morning, Ms. Standish. Can I help you?"

"Is Benjamin here?" The woman pushed into the kitchen, her gaze darting about the room before pausing at the breakfast dishes. Two plates, two cups. A knowing look crossed her face and her eyes narrowed.

"No, he's gone into town."

"Well, that's a shame. I'm here to see about his carving." She began to walk towards the back room.

Eugenie hurried after her. "I know he's still working on one more. He said it's almost done."

"Lovely, but it's the bust I want to see." She pulled the cover off the carving and tugged out a tape measure.

"What are you doing?"

"Double checking the size." She measured the height, width and depth before nodding. "As I suspected, it will work perfectly."

"For what?"

"The centrepiece of his show."

"Ben's told you he doesn't want to display it."

"What Benjamin wants and what he needs aren't necessarily the same thing."

"But—"

"This will bring him the attention he deserves, showcase what he's truly capable of."

"I'm sure he—"

"Now listen to me." Ms. Standish fixed her with a hard stare. "Do you or do you not want him to succeed?"

"Of course I want him to succeed! I was the one who got the whole ball rolling."

"Exactly. And I'm going to ensure that ball remains in motion." She picked up the carving and brushed by, forcing Eugenie to take a step back.

"Ben won't be happy." Once again, she found herself hurrying after the woman.

"He'll fuss and grumble, that's what men do. In the end, he'll thank me." Ms. Standish gave her a smile that didn't reach her eyes.

"Please…" She put her hand on the woman's arm and was rewarded with a glare.

"Take your hand off me!"

"Sorry." She pulled back surprised at the woman's sharp tone. Chip appeared at her side and growled.

"That animal is vicious!" Ms. Standish backed away.

"No, he isn't. Really." Eugenie bent and placed her arms around Chip, petting him soothingly.

"Hmph!" The woman gave Chip a wary look before turning on her heel and leaving.

Eugenie watched her drive away, a sinking feeling in her stomach. Ben wasn't going to be happy, she was sure of it. Why hadn't she done something more to stop the woman? She could have...well, there really wasn't a lot she could have done that wouldn't have exposed her as not being human.

Giving Chip a final pat, she rose to her feet and returned to the kitchen to start the dishes. It was probably her imagination that the sun wasn't shining as brightly as it had been moments earlier.

That evening, she stood in front of the dresser mirror looking at her reflection with a critical eye. The time spent watching fashion videos on her tablet had been worth it. Her dress was simple but flattering to her figure; black with a sweetheart neckline, the bodice overlaid with lace ending in short sleeves. There was definitely a knack to wearing the right clothes and she thought she had been quite successful for her first try. Her mind wandered back to the last time she went to an art show at a gallery. Then, she'd been the ugly duckling; was she now a swan? No, perhaps not a swan but certainly a handsome bird of some description.

Her appearance gave her some confidence, but she was still nervous. So much so that her stomach was churning away. What would Ben say when he saw the sculpted image of her on display after having said he didn't want to sell it? He had insisted it not be included despite Ms. Standish saying it deserved to have a place of pride. She should warn him before they got to the gallery.

A glance at her watch showed Ben would be arriving soon. She'd told him she would meet him there but he'd insisted on picking her up. As if her thoughts had conjured him, she heard the sound of his truck pulling up out front. After giving her appearance a final glance, she hurried to open the door. From the expression on Ben's face when he saw her, her dress had been a good choice. His words only confirmed her assumption.

"Eugenie, you look gorgeous."

"It's not too much?" She nervously ran her hand down the front of her dress.

"God, no. Though I doubt anyone will be looking at the artwork; all eyes will be on you."

His exaggeration created a warmth inside her and she smiled. "You look really good, too. It's the first time I've seen you in something other than jeans."

"I'd rather be in denim, covered in sawdust." He made a face and plucked at his tie. "These things aren't comfortable."

"Well, you look very handsome." She reached up and kissed him on the cheek.

Ben cleared his throat. "Well, shall we?" He gestured towards his truck.

She opened her mouth to tell him about the sculpture and then paused. It was obvious from the way he was jingling his keys that he was already nervous. Should she add to his stress? Maybe he wouldn't be too upset when he saw the carving on display. Nibbling her lip nervously, she made her way downstairs.

On entering the gallery, Eugenie had a strong sense of déjà vu. The art on the walls, people gathered in small groups, hushed laughter and the background hum of voices; it was almost exactly the same as when she'd gone to Jonathan's show. The only difference was instead of a piano there was a sound system that emitted gentle jazz. And she still felt like an outsider despite the feel of Ben's hand at the small of her back.

She relinquished her coat to a young man who gave her a numbered ticket in return which she placed in her purse. Taking a deep breath, she turned to smile at Ben only to freeze at the expression on his face.

He was angry.

No, angry was too insipid a word.

He was livid.

His eyes were almost snapping with sparks of fury.

She followed his gaze to see what had made him so enraged, although she could already guess. Sure enough, there, for all the world to see, was the carved wooden likeness of her resting on a pedestal in front of a large, and artistically arranged, display of Ben's work.

"Ah, here is one of our guests of honour, Benjamin Davis." Ms. Standish's voice rang out as she approached them. It felt like all eyes in the gallery were focused on Ben and her and, indeed, there was a soft round of applause in response to Ms. Standish's announcement.

Ben's hands clenched and unclenched at his side, his jaw clamped tightly shut. Eugenie placed her hand on his arm, silently begging him not to create a scene. Finally, he gave a small nod of acknowledgement. The crowd seemed satisfied with the gesture and returned to their private conversations. The gallery owner gave a satisfied smile and signalled to a waiter who quickly arrived with a tray of champagne flutes. Ben shook his head and Eugenie was about to do the same when Ms. Standish took two glasses off the tray and gave them no choice but to accept them.

"I see you've noticed that incredible piece of artwork of yours is displayed. I know you said you didn't want to sell it, but you never said anything about not displaying it as an example of the type of work you are capable of producing." Daphne Standish had picked up a third flute from the server's tray and took a sip from it.

Turning his back on those gathered, Ben spoke in hushed biting tones. "I thought I'd made it perfectly clear I considered that piece private and you couldn't take it." He rounded on Eugenie, his face reflecting his anger. "You knew about this, didn't you?"

"I..." She only managed to utter that one word before he continued.

"How could you have allowed it to be brought here for display?"

A sick feeling washed over her at the knowledge Ben would believe she'd betrayed his trust like that. She opened her mouth to defend her actions, but before she could say a word Ms. Standish cut across her.

"Oh, don't blame the girl. She totally lacks the sophistication to know what is passable and what is quite exceptional. You weren't available when I came by your place earlier today so I convinced your little friend here to let me take the bust." Daphne hooked her hand around Ben's arm and steered him away from Eugenie leaving her standing alone.

Once again Eugenie had a feeling of déjà vu but this time she wasn't some innocent miss floundering like a fish out of water. No standing on the sidelines for her. This time she had back up! Wandering over to a painting in which she pretended an interest, she muttered a call for Zeke under her breath. It was only a matter of minutes before a cold draught of air signalled the opening and closing of the front door and then her Heavenly friend and colleague was standing at her side.

"You called, Babe?"

She turned to look at him and her jaw dropped. The usually dark-haired angel had blond streaks and a diamond twinkled in one ear. "What have you done to yourself, Zeke?"

"Your man saw me in my natural state as the snow plow guy so I thought I should disguise myself a bit. What's up?"

"I don't know. Something doesn't feel right. The owner of the gallery, Ms. 'Call me Daphne' Standish makes my skin crawl. She's up to something and I could do with some help figuring out what."

"Which one is she?"

"The blonde with her arm hooked through Ben's as if she's afraid he might escape her."

Zeke grinned as he turned his back on the room and faced Eugenie. "I think I know why your skin is crawling."

"You do? Why?"

"I think you've had a visit from a certain green-eyed monster."

Eugenie stared at her fellow GA. Did he mean what she thought he meant? "Are you saying I'm jealous?"

"If the hat fits…"

She fell silent as she searched her inner feelings. Was she jealous? Or was there something else bothering her? Looking up into Zeke's handsome face she decided the only way he could help her was if she was absolutely truthful with him. "Perhaps, if I'm honest with myself, I am a little jealous. But I'm fairly certain it's not what's causing my unease." She stopped and tapped her lips with her forefinger as she considered Ms. Standish. "When I stand near her, I get an odd feeling. Almost as if there's evil in the vicinity. No, not evil exactly but I don't know how else to explain it."

"Babe, your GA instincts are starting to develop. Never disregard those *feelings*. Tell you what, I'll have a wander and see what I can pick up. After all, as I've mentioned before, I was created to be a GA, not a human, therefore my instincts are in-built." He patted her on the shoulder as he left her side to mingle.

Eugenie sipped at her champagne and examined the various paintings hung on the walls while surreptitiously keeping tabs on Zeke and Ben. It *did* hurt that Ben had left her to her own devices even if he hadn't left her of his own accord. And, as far as she could tell, he hadn't tried to escape Ms. Standish's clutches. Should she just march up to him or wait for him to come back to her?

It felt like hours, but, in reality, it was probably only fifteen minutes or so before Zeke returned to her side.

He grabbed a glass of champagne from a passing waiter and took a large swallow before starting to talk. "Well, you were spot on, Babe, with your feeling that there's something not quite right about that Standish woman. The vibe I'm getting isn't evil, however she *is* covering up something. And, no, it's not that she's out to steal your man. Although there's some of that, too. It's more like there's not just art sales and deals going on here."

"She's considerably older than Ben. He can't possibly want to be with her, could he?"

"Oh Babe, how old are you?"

"You know my age doesn't factor into anything."

"I'm just ribbing you, Eugenie. Yes, she's got to be at least fifteen years older than him. But I don't think you have anything to worry about; he's not interested in her other than as an art dealer."

"Good. I don't want him to get hurt." She watched Daphne Standish leave Ben's side to go and talk to a well-dressed grey-haired man whose very stance screamed wealth. "What do you think is going on then, if it's not only art that's being sold here?"

"I have absolutely no idea. I think I should do some invisible snooping. I'll get back to you as soon as I can."

Eugenie watched Zeke leave the gallery and seconds later watched him walk through a wall back into the showroom, invisible to the humans present but very obvious to her angelic eyes. He winked at her as he unfurled his wings and hovered over the heads of the guests.

Thinking he would need some time to do some eavesdropping, she went to where Ben was standing in front of the display of his artwork. He was finally free of Ms. Standish and Eugenie hoped she'd be able to talk to him, explain about how the carving had ended up in the show.

"It must be exciting to see your name on an exhibit."

"It would be, if it wasn't being spoiled by Ms. Standish's constant nagging about the carving of your ancient relative."

"Nagging?"

"She wants me to sell it." He said the word 'sell' as if it left a bad taste in his mouth.

"Sell?"

"Yes." He barely glanced at her but his eyes were cold. "I still can't believe you allowed her to take it."

"I didn't exactly *allow* her take it." She tried to explain.

"But you didn't stop her either, did you?"

"I..." She replayed the encounter in her head. She'd tried her best to stop the woman...hadn't she? Taking a deep breath, she relayed the event to Ben. "Ms. Standish appeared and started talking and somehow before I knew what was happening, she was leaving with it. You weren't there and she promised it would only be used for promotion."

He looked away, his mouth tightly compressed.

An actual pain seemed to appear in the region of her heart. "I *am* sorry, Ben. Maybe I should have done more to stop her." She placed her hand on his arm but he shook it off.

Zeke appeared by her side, visible and audible only to her. She gave him a quizzical look and he grinned back at her.

"I overheard Blondie say that your wooden alter ego is the perfect size, that it fits the requirements exactly. Any idea what that means?"

Eugenie cast a meaningful look towards Ben and gave a barely perceptible shake of her head.

Zeke nodded. "Right. You can't talk now. Listen, I'm still on assignment and I have to check on something this evening. I'll catch you later."

He disappeared and she returned her attention to Ben, tentatively touching his arm. "Ben, maybe we should leave?"

"I'm not leaving until she closes the gallery this evening. I'm not moving from this spot and I'm not letting this," he indicated the sculpture with a stabbing finger, "out of my sight. If you want to leave, go."

"I don't want to go. I..." She took a deep breath. "Ben, I've apologized. I don't know what more you want from me." She fought to keep her temper under control and remain reasonable. "She can't sell it without your permission, can she?"

"That's what I told Daphne but she pointed out the contract I signed—which your lawyer friend said was legit, by the way—states anything I agreed to display in the gallery could be sold."

"But you didn't agree to display this." She gestured at her wooden likeness.

"Exactly!" He scowled and rubbed the back of his neck before giving a decisive nod. "You know what? We *are* leaving and I'm taking *my* sculpture with me. Screw the contract! Now where's that damned Standish woman?"

Chapter 15

Ben glanced around the gallery, being tall enough to see over the heads of most of those gathered. "There she is, at the back talking to some woman who's drowning in jewellery." He started to weave between the guests leaving Eugenie to tag along if she wished.

"Ms. Standish, thank you for the evening. It's been...interesting...to say the least. We'll be leaving now and I'm taking the sculpture of the woman's head with me." He turned to go but the gallery owner's hand shot out and caught his arm.

"Mr. Davis, Benjamin, you can't go yet. Let me introduce you to Mrs. Devon. She's very interested in your carvings – especially that bust."

"Nice to meet you, Mrs. Devon, but despite what you've been led to believe that piece is *not* for sale." He ignored Mrs. Devon's extended hand and left without another word. He managed to walk half way to where his work was displayed before Daphne Standish caught up with him, grabbing his arm to stop his progress.

"Benjamin, that was incredibly rude, walking away from Mrs. Devon like that." She hissed the words to him, her voice barely above a whisper. "She's a very wealthy woman, exactly the kind of patron you need."

He shook off her grip. "I don't give a damn who she is. I'm taking my *private* artwork and going home."

"Benjamin," she gave him a tight smile. "The bust stays *here*. If you try to leave with it, I have several security guards who will be only too happy to detain you while I call the police."

He glanced about, for the first time noticing the guards posted at the doors. They weren't exactly body builders and he could probably take them on but a public brawl wouldn't do him, or his business, any good. Plus, there were a lot of people here; someone could get hurt, artwork damaged. He slowly curled his hands into fists, barely containing his frustration.

"I can see you're coming to your senses." There was a smugness to Standish's voice. "I *will* sell the carving, probably tonight. Several buyers have expressed interest. Don't worry, you'll make a nice profit from the deal."

"And I told you it's *not* for sale. You took it without my knowledge."

"And I say your little friend gave it to me."

"I didn't give it to you," Eugenie piped up standing near his elbow. He'd been so incensed, he hadn't even noticed her.

Ms. Standish raised a finely pencilled brow. "You allowed me to walk away with it. Consent was implied." She gave her hand a negligent wave. "What's done is done. And, as I said earlier, according to our contract if it's on display I can sell it."

"No. It says that anything I *agreed* to display is available for sale. *I* never agreed to display this carving."

"My dear Benjamin, don't be so naïve. Do you really want to challenge me on this? I have a very good lawyer who would tie you up in knots."

Eugenie plucked at his sleeve. "Ben, remember, I have a good lawyer friend who will help you, pro-bono."

He turned a furious look on her. "Stay out of this, Eugenie. It's your fault I might lose this carving."

"Benjamin, don't you think your future career is more important than this one piece?" Ms. Standish spoke in an overly reasonable tone. "I can do things for you.

Introduce you to the right sort of people." She flicked a look at Eugenie before reaching out and smoothing her hand down his lapel with a knowing smile. "You just have to learn to play the game."

He pointedly removed the woman's hand from his chest, while shaking his head. So like his ex. It made him want to puke. With a final glare at Ms. Standish, he took Eugenie's arm and almost dragged her to get their coats and then outside into the freezing night.

Women, they couldn't be trusted. Standish was twisting things to suit herself, blowing hot and cold as she tried to coerce him. And Eugenie saying she tried to stop Standish. Sure. Just like his ex had tried to fend off the advances of his business partner. He snorted in disgust as he unlocked the truck.

Lies, all lies.

Eugenie climbed in the truck and barely managed to put on her seatbelt before Ben drove off. He was fuming. He had no right to be angry with her, it's not as if she'd given the sculpture away to be displayed on purpose. Her only failing was being too trusting. She'd believed that woman when she'd said it was for promotional purposes – advertising Ben's capabilities in the hope of securing future commissions.

The drive to her apartment wasn't far but the stony silence between them made it feel like it took forever. When they arrived at her building she turned to Ben hoping they could kiss and make up. After the night before, she couldn't believe they'd sunk to this level.

"Goodnight." She paused her hand on the door.

Ben gave a sharp nod, staring out of the windshield.

"Should I stop by at the usual time tomorrow?"

His hands tightening on the steering wheel was the only reply he gave. Feeling tears welling in her eyes, she exited the vehicle.

Unlike all other nights, he didn't wait to make sure she was safely inside, driving off as she stood on the sidewalk. Perhaps the knowledge he no longer cared for her safety was what broke the dam on her tears. By the time she'd climbed the stairs, she was a mess, barely able to see to fit the key in the lock and let herself into her apartment.

Sniffling and hiccupping, she kicked off her shoes and dropped her bag on the table before taking off her coat and throwing it over the back of a chair. Leaving the light off, she made her way to her bedroom. The ache inside her was almost unbearable and all she wanted was the comfort of her pyjamas.

Her reflection in the mirror caught her attention. Tears stained her face, her skin looked blotchy and... She stared at the dress she'd been so pleased with mere hours ago. Now, it would always be a reminder of the most awful night of her life. She tugged it off and threw it in the corner.

"Stupid dress. Stupid art show." She muttered angrily as she donned her soft pyjamas before padding to the kitchen. She didn't drink very often but tonight she wanted a glass of wine. The only problem was she knew she didn't have any. With a little bit of concentration, a bottle of Merlot appeared on the counter already uncorked. Glass and bottle in hand she settled in an armchair in the living room hoping to numb the pain in her heart.

She was on her third glass when Zeke appeared.

"Why are you sitting in the dark?"

Blinking, she tried to focus on the tall and suddenly very sexy angel. Strange how she hadn't noticed that before. But... "Aren't you supposed to knock first before coming in?"

"I did. You didn't answer."

"Oh." She stared down into her glass. Zeke had asked her a question but she couldn't recall what it was. Something about sitting in the dark?

A table lamp switched on and by its light she watched Zeke come towards her and hunker down in front of her armchair.

"What's wrong, Babe?"

"Why would you think something is wrong?" She wiped her eyes and tried to sit up straighter.

He didn't speak, merely giving her a skeptical look. Her bravado crumpled and she allowed herself to slump in her chair once again.

"I'm drowning my sorrows." She stared into her glass before lifting it to take another drink, but he plucked it from her hand.

"I think you've had enough."

"No. Not until I'm so drunk I can't remember or care about this evening." She reached for the glass but he held it further away.

"Nope. I'm not going to let you go there." Her wine glass was suddenly replaced by a tumbler of water and he pressed it into her hand. "Drink up and then I'll get you some strong coffee to help you sober up."

"Why? I don't want to sober up." She really didn't but knew she needed to. Seeing Zeke reminded her she was a GA and she needed to be brave and resolute and...well...there was a whole list of qualities in the handbook, but at the moment she couldn't recall them all. Regardless, she obediently drank the water and then exchanged the glass for a steaming mug of coffee that had appeared on the side table.

She cradled the cup in her hands, morosely sipping the contents. "Why are you being so good to me, Zeke? I'm a terrible guardian angel. This was my first big assignment and I messed it up."

"First off, you're not a terrible GA, you've got a heart of gold which is full of love. Second... Well, helping you has made me look at myself and realise I'm capable of far more than I gave myself credit for."

His comment surprised her. "Zeke, how could you ever think of yourself as not being capable? You—"

He held up a hand, shaking his head. "Confession time here. For a long time, I was pretty hopeless as a GA. I tried too hard. I was awkward...still am at times." He shrugged. "But you...you looked up to me so I took you under my wing. I feel kinda responsible for you and that responsibility has changed me. It's been like a rite of passage."

"Really? I'd never have guessed that."

"Yeah, well, enough about me." Zeke looked uncomfortable, perhaps regretting his revelation. He got up from the floor and pulled over a chair. "We need to talk about your assignment and the twist it seems to have taken."

"Twist?"

"Yeah. But I'm not going to explain until you are completely sober. How much have you had to drink this evening?"

"There was the champagne at the gallery, I don't remember how much I drank. And then I was working on my third glass of Merlot when you arrived."

"You're a real lightweight when it comes to alcohol, Babe. You need to take it easy. Okay?"

She nodded and then took another sip of the steaming hot coffee. "I think my head is clear enough now."

"No, it isn't. Not yet at any rate. Tell me what happened to make you so miserable while we wait for the coffee to kick in."

"Ben's angry with me." She felt the tears well up again and tried to blink them away. "Ms. Standish stopped by his place today while he was gone. I let her in and before I knew what was happening she convinced me that she should take his carving of me and include it in the show this evening."

"Ben wasn't happy?"

"No. Just the opposite. And then that awful woman told him she would sell it if she got a buyer. He blames me for allowing her to take it. He didn't even kiss me when he brought me home." She knew the tears were now streaming down her cheeks but she did nothing to stop them. "I thought after we made love last night we would… Oh, I don't know what I thought."

Zeke handed her a tissue and she wiped her face then twisted it in her hand as she continued her explanation.

"I guess for a while I thought we could have a relationship. Of course, that can't be; I'll have to leave sooner or later and go back to Heaven. And then I'll be given another assignment..." Her voice trailed off as she realized she didn't want another assignment. She wanted to stay with Ben, except now Ben didn't want her anymore.

"Hmm..." Zeke wrinkled his brow. "So, to summarize. You've become intimate with a client and it means more to you than it should? Eugenie, sweetheart, you're not human. If you want a relationship, you have to find an angel."

"I know!" With that admission, she dissolved into a puddle of tears, her sobs becoming so pronounced that Zeke stood, picked her up in his arms and settled down in the armchair with her on his lap. She turned within the comfort of his arms and cried into his chest, feeling as if her heart was bleeding.

Eventually, she was spent and gave a deep sigh, having no tears left to shed.

"Are you done? Or do you have more tears you need to let out?"

She could feel Zeke's hand stroking her hair, the rhythmic movement soothing. "Sorry I made your shirt wet."

"No problem." He waved his hand and the material suddenly dried.

"Neat trick."

"Thanks." He grinned before continuing. "Listen, we need to find out what is going on with your Ms. Standish."

"She's not *my* Ms. Standish."

Zeke ignored her comment. "Get yourself dressed."

"Why?"

"There was something fishy going on at that gallery and it wasn't just the seafood hors d'oeuvres. We're going to do some after hours snooping."

"Isn't that illegal?"

"Only if we get caught, which we won't." He rubbed his hands together looking altogether too pleased with himself.

A short time later Eugenie found herself inside the art gallery with Zeke. There was no music, no crowd, no fancy spot lighting shining on the art work, just a few security lights illuminating the space enough to allow them to move about without fear of bumping into something.

"Won't we set off the alarms being in here?" She whispered the words to Zeke.

"Nah. Not as long as we are in our angelic forms."

"Right." She nodded. She should have figured that out herself. After all, they'd walked through the wall to get inside. Taking a deep breath, she tried to calm her nerves. This was too much like breaking and entering to sit well with her. Nevertheless, her job was to help Ben and if that involved sneaking into buildings at night, well then she'd do it!

As they passed through the main part of the gallery, she noticed there was a 'sold' sticker on the carving of her head. Ben was going to be furious! She was going to mention the sale to Zeke but he was already heading to the back office. She hurried to catch up with him only to bump smack into him as he came to a dead stop.

"What's wrong?"

"Eugenie, maybe we should wait or even come back later."

She was about to ask why when moaning sounds came from the office.

"Zeke, it sounds like someone is in pain in there!" She walked through the wall leaving Zeke in the gallery. One look at what was going on made her retrace her footsteps back to her colleague.

"Not what you were expecting, huh, Babe?"

"Er… No."

"Doing the deed or just getting ready?"

"Umm… Sort of neither. I've heard of that act but never seen it performed before."

"This, I gotta see." Zeke walked through the wall just as a shriek emitted from the office. Seconds later, he returned to her side. "He must be pretty good or she's a great actress because that was quite a finish."

Soon a series of electronic beeps sounded from somewhere towards the back of the gallery.

"That's the alarm being set. Blondie has probably taken her plaything security guard somewhere more comfortable, or perhaps now that she's been satisfied she's sent him home to mama. I wouldn't put either past her."

Knowing the coast was clear, they floated through the wall into the office. The first thing to catch Eugenie's eye was a pair of shocking pink lacy panties lying on the floor. She carefully stepped over them and headed to the desk while Zeke started going through the files in a tall four-drawer cabinet by the back wall.

"Zeke, do you think it's safe for me to materialize in here so I can handle things?"

He pointed up at a corner of the room. "Nope, CCTV. You don't want to get your face on YouTube, Babe. If you see anything worth investigating further, yell and I'll come check it out."

"But won't that CCTV pick up things moving on their own?"

"Yes, but it will be put down to a poltergeist phenomenon and be a five-minute wonder."

She studied the surface of the desk. "What exactly are we looking for?"

He gave a one shouldered shrug. "I'm not sure. Anything that seems unusual or that gets your senses twitching."

"Okay." Senses twitching. She wasn't quite sure what that meant but began to look. During her years in Heaven, she'd taken to reading mystery novels—the sort her parents never would have approved of—and now she felt like one of the heroines in those books hunting for clues. Where to begin?

Paperclips, a stapler, some mail that appeared to be bills. "Zeke, if there's a flashing light on the computer, does that mean it's switched on?"

"Probably. Let me look." He opened the lid on the laptop and swiped a finger on the touchpad. "Stupid woman doesn't have her computer set up to require a password when it wakes up. Look at this. She's even still logged into her email account.

Eugenie peered over Zeke's shoulder as he tapped some keys and a message appeared on the screen. She scanned the words displayed, then gave a soft gasp. Right there in front of her was a description of the bust and its dimensions. There was also a note that it was made of wood and could be easily hollowed out.

"Ben's sculpture is mentioned!"

"Hmm..." He read the complete document and then stroked his chin thoughtfully. "The original message appears to be instructions outlining what Ms. Standish needs to be looking for; various types of art work, the dimensions required and the date they have to be delivered by."

"For collectors?"

"Perhaps..." He tapped some keys, read a bit more and then leaned back grinning. "Good work, Eugenie. You found exactly what we were looking for."

"I did?" She smiled, pleased to have helped but not sure exactly what she'd done.

"Yep. Based on what I just read and what I overheard during the show earlier, I suspect Ms. Standish is a bona fide art dealer, but she does a little business on the side, helping to find artwork in which stolen items or contraband can be hidden."

"I don't understand."

"Consider this; when an item is stolen, the thief needs to find a buyer, right? Or someone might want to acquire some contraband, drugs, a precious piece of antiquity or art. It seems there's an organization that facilitates that. They put buyers and sellers together. Then they ship the item to the purchaser."

"How do they get the shipments past customs? I'm sure I've read about sniffer dogs and parcels being inspected."

"They hide the items in artwork. A famous painting can be hidden behind the canvas of a local artist. Jewels or drugs with scented herbs to confuse the dogs can be secreted inside sculptures...or perhaps inside a wooden carving of a woman's head.

Eugenie let out a soft gasp. "So that's why Ms. Standish is so anxious to keep Ben's work. It's going to be used to smuggle something!"

"Yep. According to some of these emails it seems there's a network of small art galleries around the country that receive lists of requirements each month. They then know what sizes and types of artwork to look out for. When they find one that is suitable, they contact the facilitating organization and the piece is bought. Up to that point, it's legitimate. The galleries aren't breaking any laws, but perhaps a good lawyer could make a case for abetting in a crime."

"I have to tell Ben. He'll be horrified." She turned to leave.

"Wait a minute there, Eugenie. It's the middle of the night and besides that, how are you going to explain to your man how you know all this?"

"Oh. I didn't think."

"I don't see a way you could tell him what's going on without explaining how you found out." Zeke drummed his fingers on the desk.

After a few minutes of silence, he looked up with a smile on his face. "I think I know how we can sort this out. I'll have to get permission from Michael but I don't see him objecting."

"What are you going to do?" Eugenie looked at him expectantly.

"Best you don't know so you can react naturally when the information is relayed to Ben. Tomorrow, I think you should go over to his place and try to apologise. Whatever you do, don't let on you know anything about Ms. Standish's side business. Okay?"

Chapter 16

Ben sat on his sofa, a shot of whiskey in his hand. Unlike recent evenings, there was no warmth from a fire, no friendly crackle of burning logs or flickering light casting interesting shadows on the wall. The room was cold and dark which matched his mood perfectly.

The entire evening had been a disaster. From the moment he'd put on that stupid suit and tie he'd felt uncomfortable, memories of his failed marriage plaguing him. His ex had bought it for him to wear to one of her ridiculous parties. It had cost an arm and a leg, money he'd begun to realize he no longer had. The business had been bleeding money for some reason though he hadn't yet discovered why. Then, at the party he'd stepped outside to get some air only to find his wife and his supposed friend and business partner locked in a very intimate embrace in the gazebo. That had been the end of it; he'd moved out that night, filed for divorce the next day.

So yeah, putting on the suit had started the night on a downward spiral. He'd tried to pull out of it for Eugenie's sake, knowing she was excited about the evening but the minute he'd stepped into the gallery everything had crashed and burned. The one carving he'd said should never be displayed was sitting there prominently for everyone to see.

It was a betrayal of his trust, almost like reliving the end of his marriage all over again. Except this was worse. His love—no, make that infatuation—for his wife had died long before that last night, but Eugenie... He'd thought she was different. He should have known better.

"How many times do I have to be kicked in the teeth before I learn my lesson?" He took another mouthful of whisky and then focused his gaze on the portrait hanging over the mantle. He and Eugenie had spent so many evenings in this very spot and he'd always felt the portrait had watched over them, giving them its blessing so to speak. What a fool he'd been. She was no better than the rest, saying one thing while meaning another, going behind his back, out for his money. He wouldn't be surprised to learn Standish was giving her a cut of the proceeds from the sale of the carvings.

Realizing his glass was empty, he picked up the bottle and poured out more, carelessly slopping the booze over the edge. Damn. He stumbled to the kitchen to get a dishrag to clean up the spill. A few months ago, he wouldn't have bothered, but Eugenie had worked so hard to tidy up the place, he was...

He paused, frowning. Why had she done all that cleaning for him? He ran his hand through his hair as he looked around. The whole house sparkled and had a warm, cared for vibe that had been missing for ages. There were even homemade cookies in a tin on the counter; she'd found an old recipe book of his mother's, and when he'd mentioned his mother's oatmeal cookies, Eugenie had made some for him as a surprise.

It didn't make sense. He'd not paid her for any of the work, hadn't even asked her to do it. She'd taken it upon herself, seeming to go out of her way to make him happy. And last night... He groaned thinking of how they'd had sex. No, it hadn't been sex; they'd made love. He'd had meaningless sex before, scratching the itch, but last night had been so much more. He'd felt a connection to her that went way beyond the physical.

Feeling tired beyond words, he sank down into a chair at the kitchen table and propped his head in his hands. Had he messed up? He'd been incensed when he'd seen that sculpture, assuming Eugenie had been in collusion with Daphne Standish. So caught up in his own feelings, he hadn't really listened to her explanation.

"Oh hell, what have I done?"

His alarm clock was ringing, the sound oddly distant but still loud enough it was pounding into his brain. Ben reached out his hand to turn it off but couldn't locate it. Groaning, he opened his eyes and realized he was in the kitchen, sleeping with his head on the table.

He sat up, cursing as his neck and back protested the position he'd been in. Sunlight was streaming through the window, and he squinted as he pushed himself to his feet and stumbled down the hall to his bedroom. After shutting off the alarm, he went to the bathroom and paused when he caught a glimpse of himself in the mirror. Bloodshot eyes, his hair standing up on end and he was still wearing that damned suit.

Once the shower was running, he ditched the suit leaving it crumpled on the floor and stepped under the pounding water, hoping it would help him wake up. He hadn't been hung over since the second time Eugenie appeared on his doorstep and, speaking of her, he needed to apologize for his behaviour last night. Hopefully, if he grovelled enough, he'd be able to get her to listen. Damn, he'd really screwed up, big time!

He was on his second cup of coffee when he glanced out the window and saw Eugenie walking up the driveway. His mug halfway to his mouth, he froze not believing she was actually here. Given the way he'd treated her both at the gallery and afterwards on the way back to her apartment, he wouldn't have been surprised if she'd refused to set foot in his place ever again. He'd thought he would have to drive into town and then hope she wouldn't slam her door in his face.

She tapped on the door. His feet dragged as he went to let her in, anticipating a barrage of well-deserved condemnations.

"Good morning, Ben." She looked up at him tentatively.

"Eugenie, I can't believe you're here."

"I said I'd be here at the usual time but if you don't want me—"

"No!" He almost shouted the word and when she took a step back, he reached out and took her arm, guiding her inside. "I want you here. I mean, I know I was a complete bastard last night and I can't believe you'd even want to breathe the same air as me."

She shrugged and looked away. He could tell her feelings were still hurt but at least she hadn't completely shut him out. There was still a chance.

"Eugenie, I'm sorry about last night." He took her hands in his. "I was way out of line. Baggage from the past messed with my thinking and I reacted instinctively rather than listening to your explanation."

"I..." She looked down at the ground, hesitated as if considering what to say and then peered up at him, emotion evident in her eyes. "You really hurt me last night, Ben."

"I know. I'm a total ass." He took a deep breath. "I was going to drive into town to see you this morning, beg you to forgive me. I know that Daphne woman is pushy and she probably steamrolled right over you."

She nodded. "That's pretty much what happened."

"When I saw that image of you, I felt betrayed. The whole scenario was so reminiscent of the kinds of things that used to happen with my ex-wife. I was taking it all out on you. I should have realized you'd never do something like that."

"You can't let the past shape your future."

"I know." He made a self-deprecating face. "It won't happen again, I promise. Will you give me a second chance?"

She nodded. "I'll give you another chance, but I think I need some time before I can be as close to you as I have been." She pulled her hands from his and he winced, already missing the connection they'd had before.

"Thanks. From now on, I'll try and leave my past where it belongs…in the past."

She gave a half-smile and turned to look out the window. "It's really gloomy out today."

"Yep." He followed her lead. "It will probably snow again later."

"Good thing the show was last night then. If the weather was bad, there might not have been such a good turn out."

"There *were* a lot of people there, weren't there?"

"Did you notice some of your smaller carvings had sold stickers on them?"

"Really? No, I didn't. I was too riled up about that sculpture being there to notice anything else," he slid a glance her way wondering how she'd react to him mentioning his bad behaviour. Her expression remained calm and he let out a silent breath, relieved they seemed to have moved past any recriminations. "That's great, though. About the sales, I mean. I didn't think anyone would want them."

She smiled and shook her head at him. "Ben, you really *are* talented. When are you going to believe that?"

He shrugged. "I don't know. I guess it will take a while to sink in."

"Well, in the meantime, remember that I believe in you." She pressed her hand to his chest and he covered it with his, holding it in place.

"You really are amazing, Eugenie. Most women would have yelled or thrown something at me or refused to talk."

"I think you've been associating with the wrong sort of women."

"Maybe. Or maybe you're unique, my own special gift from God."

For some reason, she stiffened at his words but before he could ask why, there was a knock on the door.

"I wonder who that could be? Chip didn't bark." He opened the door to see a tall young man standing on the porch with his back to the door. "Can I help you?" The man turned around and Ben thought he looked familiar.

"Benjamin Davis?"

"Yes." He answered cautiously.

The man took a badge out of his pocket. "Detective-Constable Ezekiel Andrews, RCMP. You might have noticed me at the gallery last evening."

"No, I didn't." He frowned and checked Andrews' identification. It seemed real enough. "What can I do for you?"

"I'm here about the art show."

Eugenie came to the door and touched Ben's arm. "You're letting all the heat out. Why don't you come inside and explain."

Ben raised his brows at her. He wasn't keen on letting the man in the house, his instincts telling him something was off though he wasn't sure what. However, he opened the door wider to allow Andrews to enter and gestured towards the kitchen.

"Now, what's all this about the art show?" Ben leaned against the kitchen counter, arms folded.

"We've been following several lines of investigation concerning the sale of various stolen property and one of those lines has led us to the Maple Leaf Gallery." The detective placed his badge back in his pocket as he spoke.

He shook his head. "None of my work has been stolen; it was all on show quite legitimately. Apart from one piece which I hadn't given permission to be displayed, but I still wouldn't deem that stolen."

"Which piece would that be, sir?" The officer pulled out a notepad and pen.

"A bust, a carved wooden head and shoulders of a woman."

"Ah." He wrote something down, nodding, then flipped the notebook shut. "That's the exact piece we're interested in."

Out of Ben's line of sight, Eugenie rolled her eyes at Zeke. Firstly, she couldn't believe he had the nerve to impersonate a member of the Royal Canadian Mounted Police. Secondly, his performance made her think of a show she'd seen while flipping through television channels a few nights back. Hoping Ben hadn't watched the same show, she took a seat at the table so she could hear Zeke's explanation.

"Let me give you a brief overview so you have a sense of what we're dealing with." Zeke pulled out a chair, turned it to face backwards and sat down, hands clasped on the back of it. "When a thief steals something he needs to find a buyer, right? Now, sometimes he'll go to a well-known fence. Occasionally that fence is a pawnbroker or...an art dealer."

"An art dealer?" Ben frowned.

Zeke nodded. "Yes. Someone at the Maple Art Gallery to be exact."

Eugenie felt her lips twitching at Zeke's expression. He was trying so hard to be serious, like one of those police officers she'd seen on TV. She needed to get away before she burst out laughing. "Excuse me for interrupting, but would you like a hot drink, Detective?"

"That's okay, ma'am, I'm fine." Zeke shot her a faintly annoyed look. "As I was saying, we've been investigating the sale of stolen property. What we know so far is that there is a network of legitimate small galleries and art dealers around the world who receive requests for certain types of artwork with specific dimensions. When such a piece is found by a dealer it's bought legally by an organization for a large sum, often more than it's worth. It is then taken to a clearing house somewhere in Canada where a stolen item is hidden within the artwork and then shipped across borders to a buyer."

"I don't see how I can be of use." Ben pushed off from where he was leaning on the counter and poured himself a cup of coffee. "None of my carvings are big enough to hide much of anything."

"Except the sculpture, Ben." Eugenie corrected him from where she stood at the sink, supposedly filling the kettle for tea.

"That's correct." Zeke nodded. "I was at the gallery last night and saw the piece in question. We think it fits the requirements on a recent list that has come into our hands."

"Damn." Ben's hand tightened around the cup he was holding. "That would explain why Ms. Standish was so fired up to have that damned carving in her gallery even though I repeatedly told her it was *not* for sale."

Zeke cleared his throat. "Yes, I managed to overhear some of that conversation. However, we strongly suspect you will be contacted by the gallery today with the news it has been sold."

"What?" Ben slammed his mug down on the counter. "I'll be damned if I'll let a bunch of criminals use my art work—"

Zeke interrupted. "Actually, the RCMP would like you to do just that. We'd like you to inform Daphne Standish that you've changed your mind about selling the piece, with one proviso."

"Which is?" Ben folded his arms across his chest.

"That you get to meet the buyer in person first."

"How will that help?"

"We can tail him when he leaves the gallery, track the carving and with luck shut down this branch of the operation."

Ben grunted, his brows lowered as considered the proposal. "They'd better not damage it."

"We will make every effort to return the carving back to you in one piece." Zeke stood up. "Can we count on you?"

Ben sighed. "Yeah, all right. I'll do it."

Zeke held out his hand for Ben to shake. "Thank you, Mr. Davis. We will be in touch once we have news."

Chapter 17

After Zeke left, they fell back into their usual routine, heading out to the barn to work. Snow was falling gently, creating a fresh white blanket over the farm.

"It looks like a Christmas card outside," Eugenie decided as she peered out the window.

Ben looked up from the table he was working on. "Yeah, I guess so."

"How do you celebrate Christmas in Canada, Ben?"

He shrugged. "Probably the same as most other places. Although, to tell you the truth, I haven't celebrated it in quite a while."

"You haven't?" She looked at him aghast. "We'll have to do something about that."

"You really do like to take charge of my life, don't you?"

"Oh." Her smile faltered. "I'm not trying to be bossy. I just want to help you."

"It's okay." He stood and walked over to where she was. "I sort of like you taking charge. My life was a mess until you appeared." He took her hands in his, seemed about to kiss her and then held back, no doubt recalling her earlier warning.

She squeezed his hands gently to let him know she still cared. "It's still a week until Christmas. We don't have to make any decisions today." She wanted to make Christmas special, not only for Ben but for herself, too. Knowing she would have to go back to Heaven soon and never see him again was going to be painful, but if she could store up some good memories.

The ringing of Ben's phone interrupted her thoughts and she watched him answer it, listen intently and occasionally grumble in agreement.

When he ended the call, he turned to her. "That was Detective Andrews. Everything is in place for the sting. We just need to get Ms. Standish to agree to a meeting between us and the buyer. Then Andrews will follow the buyer to the next link in the chain."

"Okay, do we go now?"

He shook his head. "*We* aren't going anywhere. *I'll* go by myself. This shouldn't be dangerous; but just in case, I don't want to take the chance of anything happening to you."

She planted her hands on her hips. "Don't be ridiculous. Of course, I'm going with you. I'm the one who got you involved with Ms. Standish."

"But–"

"Ben, you either take me along or..." She faltered not sure what kind of threat she could use.

"Or?" He raised one brow then laughed and pulled her close for a hug. "That's what I love about you, Eugenie. Always ready to jump in where angels fear to tread."

"Uh...right." She was glad her face was pressed to his chest so he couldn't see her expression. Sometimes Ben's comments made her wonder if he'd been as unconscious as she'd thought the day she'd rescued him in the snow.

It didn't take long to drive into town and arrive at the gallery. Ben took a deep breath as they entered the building, memories of the previous evening causing him to wince. Standish's high-handed abduction of his carving, how he'd turned on Eugenie... He gave his head a shake. Now wasn't the time to be raking over old coals. He needed to be acting conciliatory, emphasis on *acting*.

"You're back." Ms. Standish stalked across the room, a pinched look about her face, her heels making an angry staccato on the floor. "I hope you're not here to create another scene like you did last night. It was appallingly bad manners on your part."

Eugenie opened her mouth and he gave her hand a warning squeeze.

"Yes...I mean, no." He shuffled his feet. "Eugenie and I have been talking and I'll agree to you selling the bust."

"Excellent." Ms. Standish's expression changed to a smile. "I was actually going to call you today with the news that we have a buyer."

"But there's one condition." Eugenie ended his comment for him.

"And what might that be?" The woman fixed her with a pointed stare.

Ben supplied the answer. "I want to meet the buyer first."

"Impossible." Ms. Standish turned her attention back to Ben as he spoke.

"That's my condition. Take it or leave it." He folded his arms.

"No," Ms. Standish shook her head. "Many of my buyers are wealthy with extensive private collections. They don't want people to know who they are for security reasons."

He shrugged. "Then I guess I'll take the carving home with me now."

"No!"

"There are no security guards here today. No witnesses. It's your word against mine."

Ms. Standish gaped at him, likely unused to being thwarted.

Ben smiled, pleased to have the upper hand. "Eugenie, will you go get it for me, please?"

She began to walk towards where the carving was still on display.

"You can't take it." Ms. Standish hurried across the room placing herself in Eugenie's way. "We have a contract." There was a hint of panic in her voice.

"And I have a lawyer. Do you really want the negative publicity for your gallery?" He walked over and placed his hands on Eugenie's shoulders. "She's prepared to testify that you took the carving while I wasn't home and without my permission."

Eugenie nodded in agreement. "That's right. This could drag on for ages and put your business practices into question."

Ms. Standish frowned. "I..." She paused and glanced towards the back of the gallery. "This is highly unusual but I'll make a call and see if I can get the buyer to agree to your *very* irregular request."

"Thank you," he gave her a smile that didn't reach his eyes. "We'll wait here while you make the arrangements."

"You don't have to wait. I'll call you once the buyer agrees." Ms. Standish tried to usher them towards the door but they didn't move.

"As Ben said, we'll wait here." Eugenie clasped her hands around his arm. "Given our past experience with you, we're not sure you can be trusted not to spirit the sculpture away when our backs are turned."

The gallery owner's cheeks flushed and she almost trembled with indignation. "Well, I never!"

He spotted a bench. "We'll wait here." Sitting down, he stretched his legs out in front of him and folded his arms leaving Ms. Standish in no doubt he intended to stay until his conditions were met.

She gave them another frown before hurrying to the back.

"I wonder how long it will take," Eugenie whispered.

"No idea. From what Andrews said on the phone, he seemed to feel there was some kind of hub in the area."

"Okay." She glanced about the room then nodded towards the area where his work was displayed. "Did you see the sold stickers?"

"No, but I remember you mentioning them." He stood up and went to check. A smile spread across his face as he saw that Eugenie had been right. "Hey, there really are quite a few sold."

"I told you so."

"I wonder if they're legitimate sales though." His smile faded.

"I'm sure most of the business is above board. That's what Detective Andrews said anyway."

"I hope so." He mentally calculated the profits he might make from the sales. It was a tidy sum and would go a long way towards paying off some of his debt.

Ms. Standish reappeared. "I managed to convince the buyer to concede to your wishes. He wasn't pleased but regardless, he'll be here soon."

"Thank you." He gestured towards the rest of the display. "When will I be paid for these?"

"At the end of the month as per our agreement." Ms. Standish pursed her lips.

"Our agreement seems to be open to interpretation." He gave a pointed look at the bust.

"I run a respected establishment." Affronted, she turned on her heel and walked away.

Eugenie gave him a nod of approval. "Good. She knows you're keeping an eye on things."

"After being burned by my former partner, my trust level is pretty low. I'm keeping a close eye on my finances."

"Do you want to see the receipts for the items I sold for you?"

He rolled his eyes. "Of course not. I trust you."

"That's not what you said last night." As soon as she was finished speaking, she pressed her hand to her mouth. "I'm sorry. I shouldn't have said that."

He gently took her hand from her lips and kissed her fingertips. "Yes, you should have said that. I messed up big time and we can't just brush it under the rug."

"But holding a grudge and bringing up things you've already apologized for isn't right either."

He gently chucked her under the chin. "You're quite wise for someone so young."

She gave a mysterious smile that once again had him marvelling at her resemblance to the painting on his wall.

Eugenie paced the gallery for the umpteenth time. They'd been waiting over half an hour for the buyer to show up. Perhaps that wasn't a great length of time but with nothing to do but stare at the artwork it seemed longer. Ms. Standish had hinted several times that they should go next door to the coffee shop but Ben wasn't budging.

Sighing, she shifted from one foot to the other. She needed to use the washroom but didn't think Ms. Standish would be keen on letting her use the facilities. There was the option of going to the coffee shop but what if the buyer appeared while she was gone. No, she'd wait and hope he arrived soon!

She was in the process of checking her watch yet again, when the gallery door opened letting in a gust of cold air as well as a middle-aged gentleman in a black trench coat. Was this the buyer?

"Heads up, Zeke." She whispered the words before hurrying over to where Ben was slowly rising to his feet. Out of the corner of her eye she caught a glimpse of Zeke, invisible to the human eye, leaning against the far wall with his arms crossed against his chest. He touched two fingers to his forehead in a greeting and, unfolding from his stance, drifted over to where Ben, Ms. Standish and the stranger were now standing.

"This is Benjamin Davis, the artist who carved the artwork you purchased."

The man extended his hand. "John Brown. Pleased to meet you, Davis. Amazing work."

"Thanks." Ben eyed the man up and down and Eugenie did the same taking in his appearance. Average height and build, average features. Common name. The kind of person you'd pass by and not remember, which, if he was indeed a criminal, probably worked in his favour.

"I was really taken with that carving you did. Very lifelike." Mr. Brown jerked his chin towards the carving.

"It holds a special meaning to me," Ben explained as he walked over to the bust. "I've worked on it for years trying to get it right."

"You did a fine job." The buyer clasped his hands behind his back.

Ben ran a finger over the cheek of the carving and Eugenie could have sworn she actually felt his touch.

He paused and then cleared his throat. "I want you to take special care of this piece. It, and the woman who inspired it, mean more to me than I could ever put into words." Ben looked up as he spoke, his gaze moving past Brown and Standish and locking on hers.

Eugenie's heart seemed to melt in her chest and, if it hadn't been for their audience, she would have rushed over and hugged him.

Instead, Ms. Standish spoiled the moment. "Now if you're satisfied Benjamin, I'll box this up so Mr. Brown can be on his way. He's a busy man and has spared all the time he can for you."

Brown looked at his watch. "Yes, I need to be on my way."

Eugenie watched as Ben's jaw tightened. She could tell he wasn't happy about this at all. "We mustn't keep the man, Ben." She walked over and took his arm.

He glanced at her and nodded. "Of course. Thanks for allowing me to meet you. I know you'll take good care of my work."

"That I will." Mr. Brown took the box Ms. Standish handed him. "Wonderful doing business with you." With a nod, he turned and left.

Eugenie turned and saw the man get into a plain grey four-door sedan. It was as unremarkable as the man himself except for a dent in the fender. For a supposedly wealthy man, she'd have thought he'd own something more upscale. Frowning, she watched him drive away before turning back to the gallery owner and Ben.

"Well, that's taken care of." Ms. Standish rubbed her hands together. "I hope you're satisfied now, Benjamin. I'll send you a cheque with payment for this and for the other pieces at the end of the month."

"Thank you." Eugenie tugged at Ben's arm leading him towards the door. "We need to be on our way as well." Zeke had left to follow the buyer and she wanted to check in and see what was happening. Plus, she really needed to use the washroom!

Chapter 18

Ben ordered coffee while Eugenie went to use the facilities. He found a table in the corner and sat down, nursing the mug while he stared out at the street.

It was decorated for Christmas with wreaths hanging from the streetlamps and urns full of greenery and bows dotting the sidewalks. Funny how he hadn't even noticed the decorations before. But then again, since Eugenie had appeared in his life, he was seeing a lot of things that had escaped his notice before. How the light sparkled against the icicles that hung near the door to the shop, birds in trees, animal tracks in the snow. Her child-like delight in simple things was fascinating and contagious. Just the other day he'd caught himself studying the designs in the frost that coated the truck window rather than grumbling about having to scrape the windshield clear.

He sipped his coffee and shook his head. With her looks and knowledge of antiques, he was sure Eugenie would soon be off to the bright lights of the big city. There was nothing in a backwater, small town like this to hold her interest for long. Life wouldn't be the same once she was gone, though. At least he had the painting that looked like her, and the carving…provided he actually got it back.

While he wouldn't admit it to anyone, he was pretty torn up about possibly losing that sculpture. Sure, it was technically a chunk of wood but he'd put his heart into carving it. Plus, it was a tangible reminder of Eugenie. If anything happened to it, that cop was going to have hell to pay.

After leaving Ben to get coffee, Eugenie found the women's bathroom and checked all stalls were empty. Even though no one else would be able to see her angelic colleague, standing in the washroom talking to herself would definitely cause some stares. Confident the coast was clear, she contacted Zeke.

"Zeke? Where are you? What's going on?"

"Hey, Babe." He appeared beside her and glanced around the washroom. "Interesting choice of meeting venue."

"This was the only place I thought we might have a modicum of privacy."

"Modicum? Sometimes you talk like you've swallowed a dictionary, Eugenie." He chuckled as he shoved his hands in his pockets. Eugenie noticed he was wearing a dark leather jacket, ratty old jeans and had stubble showing on his jaw. It was a far cry from the clean-cut officer who had appeared on Ben's doorstep.

"Why are you dressed like that?"

"I'm an undercover cop. Gotta look the part." He slouched and changed his expression to a brooding scowl before grinning. "What do you think?"

"I think you enjoy this far too much." She folded her arms and shook her head. "What's happening with Ben's carving?"

"Right, to business. The guy, Brown, is taking it to the processing location. It's a small farm outside of town, not too far from Ben's place actually." He pulled his phone out from his jacket and showed her a map. "See?"

A rattling at the washroom door stopped her from replying and, reacting before she had time to think, she dived into a stall dragging Zeke with her.

"Eugenie, I could have just disappeared." Zeke made a face at being squished so close to her in the small space.

"Shh." She hissed. "Stay quiet until whoever is out there has left."

"I feel like some kind of pervert," Zeke muttered. "I'll be back in a minute." And just like that he disappeared.

Well, at least there was more room in the stall now, she thought to herself as she impatiently waited for the person to leave. As soon as the washroom door clicked, she exited the cubicle.

"Coast is clear, Zeke."

He reappeared with a sign in his hand. It said 'out of order'.

"What's that for?"

"To keep us from being interrupted again." With a wave of his hand, the sign seemed to flow through the door. "Now it's posted on the other side. You can take it down when you leave."

"Good idea! Now, back to the business at hand. What's going on with that Mr. Brown character and Ben's carving." She proceeded to wash and dry her hands while Zeke spoke.

"I've been in touch with the RCMP and they're on their way to the farm."

"Aren't they curious as to who you are, or did you call them anonymously?"

"Umm... I may have committed a tiny felony. I altered police records and Ezekiel Andrews is, for the time being, a bona fide detective-constable in the RCMP."

"Zeke! You didn't?"

"I'll erase all the records as soon as this is over. And I'll do some mind wipes. No one will remember me. Don't worry, Eugenie."

"I *am* worried. I'm in a constant quake thinking of possible exposure."

"You'll get used to it. You just have to think on your feet and be prepared to roll with the punches so to speak. Plus, humans are easily distracted. They're busy with their own lives and see what they expect to see. Small inconsistencies are rarely noticed."

"I suppose."

"Trust me." Zeke gave her a nod. "Now you head on back to Ben; he's going to wonder where you are. I'll zip over to the farm house and make sure the RCMP get their man or men."

"If it's at all possible, please try and protect Ben's sculpture. He's very worried about it."

"I will and I'll let you know the outcome as soon as it's all over."

"Thank you, Zeke." Eugenie stretched up on tip-toe and kissed the GA's cheek before returning to Ben who was sitting hunched over a mug with steam rising from it.

She sat down opposite him and placed her hand on his.

"Ben. It *will* be okay. You know that, don't you? You will get your work back and the police will break up the smuggling ring."

"I hope you're right, Eugenie. But I doubt I'll ever see the sculpture again, at least, not in one piece."

"You have to have faith that everything will be all right. And regardless of what happens to the carving, assisting the RCMP was the right thing to do. You couldn't live with yourself if you hadn't helped stop a crime, could you?

"I suppose not."

"You're an honourable man and it's one of the things I love about you."

"Thanks. And you always seem to see the positive side of things and I love that about you." He gave her hand a gentle squeeze.

"In the meantime, it's pointless hanging around here. Let's go back to your place. I'm sure the police will contact you when it's all over."

They drove in silence for a few miles. Ben's concern was palpable. Truth be told, she was concerned as well. Zeke, even though young in angelic terms, was a far more powerful guardian angel than she; he must have experience with danger but it was still hard to get her head wrapped around the idea. And then there was Ben's carving. It was important to him and she hoped Zeke would be able to keep it safe. The note she'd seen on the computer screen mentioning the carving
could be easily hollowed out filled her with unease.

An idea popped into her head and she decided to act on it. Maybe, just maybe, she could be of some help. If she was at least in the vicinity…

"Ben, take the next turn." She pointed to the right.

"Why?"

"Christmas is only a week away. We need to get a Christmas tree for the house, right? The road leads to a tree farm. See? There's the sign."

"I'm not in the mood for this, Eugenie. I just want to get home."

When she heard Ben say *home* she felt a pain in the region of her heart, but she pushed it aside and continued with her plan. "Please, Ben, let's go. It'll be fun and it will take your mind off things."

"I doubt that but all right, for you, I will." He made the turn.

It was a gravel road and they bumped along for some distance before she called out. "Look, Ben. Over by that farmhouse. That's the car Mr. Brown was driving; I remember that dent in the fender."

Ben slowed the vehicle and then eased over to the shoulder. A stand of trees partially obscured the view but the car was visible. "Are you sure?"

She nodded. "Positive. Let's stay and watch what happens for a while."

"Sounds good to me. I'm not sure I totally trust that cop. I kept getting a weird vibe about him. Like he wasn't exactly who he said he was."

Eugenie struggled to keep her expression from revealing her surprise. So much for Zeke saying humans didn't notice things! "Probably because he works undercover a lot."

"How would you know that?"

"Err...just a guess. Something about him..." How could Zeke ever think this became easier?

"Oh." Thankfully, Ben accepted her explanation. He switched off the engine and rested his forearms on the steering wheel. He narrowed his eyes then nodded to the left. "Look over there, beyond that group of trees."

She peered at where he'd indicated. "You mean those cars?"

"Yep. I bet those are unmarked police cars. And look over to the right, there are the cops."

Sure enough, cautiously approaching the farm house was a small contingent of men and women who seemed about to storm the house or do a takedown or whatever it was called.

A wave of nervousness washed over her. They were almost in the middle of a police operation. What if there was gunfire? Ben might get hurt. This may not have been such a good idea after all.

"Ben, I think we should leave. I—"

Just then, there was a rush of movement. One RCMP officer kicked the door down, the dull thud of his boot on the wooden surface echoing across the distance. It was immediately followed by the sound of shouting as the other members of his team rushed into the building. Eugenie barely had time to register what was happening at the front of the building when activity at the rear drew her attention. There was a crashing sound and an explosion of glass shards as Brown burst through a window like a bat out of hell. He rolled as he hit the ground, scrambled to his feet, then bolted towards the woods. Eugenie sat up straighter in her seat as she realized he was heading straight for their vehicle.

"That's him! That's the bugger who took my sculpture! Something must have tipped him off." Ben shoved his door open.

"Where do you think you're going?" Eugenie grabbed at his arm but was too late. Ben was out of the truck and running towards the buyer trying to head him off.

"Oh, hell and damnation!" Not even caring she was swearing, she tore off her seatbelt and ran after him.

The forest floor was lightly covered with snow, enough to obscure a view of the ground and she tripped and stumbled over unseen vines and branches. Ben, however, seemed to have no similar issues, his long legs carrying him across the terrain as if he was the one with wings rather than she. The gap between him and Brown became smaller and smaller and then with a yell, Ben launched himself through the air to tackle the fleeing man.

Brown turned at the sound of Ben's yell, shock showing on his face before Ben slammed into him and they both hit the ground, a shower of snow flying up into the air momentarily obscuring them from view.

Eugenie skidded to a halt and watched, wide-eyed as the two men grappled. Brown was stronger than she would have suspected and the two men struggled, rolling back and forth, eventually falling into a ditch, breaking through the thin layer of ice and soaking them both in freezing water and mud.

Brown managed to push Ben away, reached into his pocket and…pulled out a knife!

A scream ripped from her throat. "Ben, look out!"

Oh no, not Ben! Please keep him safe. The rough prayer spilled from her lips as she rushed forward with every intention of helping her lover. She didn't get far, however. A dark-haired angel dressed in black denim and white t-shirt blocked both her headlong flight and her view with his outstretched wings.

"Zeke, what are you doing? I have to help Ben. That man has a knife."

"Orders from above, Eugenie. Sorry, but we can't interfere. Ben has to face his fate head-on."

"No! To hell with orders and rules!" She feinted left then to the right and ducked under Zeke's wings. She'd deal with the punishment later. Right now, she had to save Ben!

She'd only taken a step when strong arms snaked around her waist. "Nope. I can't let you do it, Eugenie."

Like a madwoman, she pulled at the arms that held her, not caring her nails were scoring his skin. "Let me go! Please, I'm begging you." Tears blurred her vision and her words were spoken between sobs.

"Aww, Eugenie..." His resolve might have weakened in the face of her tears or maybe it was the fact that she'd resorted to a backwards kick towards his groin. Whatever the case, she was suddenly free and flying across the distance that separated her from the man she loved.

Ben had Brown's knife hand in a vise-like grip, their arms trembling with strain as they fought to overpower each other. Not sure what to do, not wanting to distract Ben lest the other man took advantage, she looked around wildly for something, anything, she could use to tip the balance in Ben's favour.

Just as she reached for a stick, thinking she'd whack it down across Brown's arm, Ben gave a roar and somehow managed to overpower his opponent. The knife slipped from Brown's fingers and Eugenie quickly kicked it out of reach.

Zeke was suddenly at her side again, pulling her away. "Jeez, Eugenie, you just broke a gazillion rules. Attacking a fellow angel. Flipping into angelic form and flying within view of humans. Attempting to interfere with fate. Michael is going to have a fit.”

“What?” She answered distractedly, watching as Brown took a swing at Ben. Ben dodged, drew back his fist and hit Brown square on the chin. The man’s head snapped back and he crumpled to the ground.

Ben grabbed the man’s collar and dragged him from the soggy ditch, dumping him on the ground.

“Perfect timing,” Zeke commented and jerked his chin towards the farmhouse. “Here come the cops.”

Sure enough, when Eugenie turned her head to look, several men were running in their direction.

“Zeke, I’m sorry if I hurt you but I couldn’t stand by and watch, doing nothing.” She managed to pull her attention away from the human activities and turned to apologize. “And I’ll take full blame and tell Michael—”

He shook his head. “Don’t fret. I did a quick mind wipe and the humans won’t recall seeing you. And as for hurting me, I’m pretty tough.” He gave her a gentle push. “Go see your man and don’t worry about me.”

Heeding Zeke’s words, she ran over to where Ben now stood shaking his hand.

“Are you all right?” She grabbed his shoulders and looked him over head to toe.

“Yeah. My hand hurts, that’s all. The guy’s got a jaw like steel!” Ben grinned and pulled her close then kissed her. “But I must say I thoroughly enjoyed hitting him.”

“Men!” She shook her head and then realized her skin was getting damp, the water from Ben’s clothing transferring to hers.

“You’re soaking wet and you’re shivering! Here,” she pulled off her coat and tried to wrap it around him. “Use my coat. It’s not much but it’s the best I can do until we get someplace warm.”

"Eugenie, I don't need..." He paused in the act of removing the coat and frowned. "'Why do I feel like we've done this before?"

"I...I've no idea." She scrambled trying to think of an explanation and breathed a sigh of relief when the cops arrived and diverted Ben's attention.

Of course, there were questions as to how they happened to be on the scene but she was able to weave a plausible tale. After all, they really had been on their way to get a tree when she'd seen the car and recognized it. A small white lie, or was that a lie of omission? At this point, she didn't really care. She just wanted to get Ben home and warm.

Chapter 19

Ben cranked up the heat in the truck. He was frozen. His teeth were chattering, his toes and fingers numb. During the fight, he hadn't noticed the cold; anger and adrenaline had kept him going. Now, however, he couldn't wait to get home and into a hot bath.

That same sense of déjà vu niggled at his brain again. It was almost a year to the day from the last time he'd ended up in water in the middle of winter. He'd been eager for a hot bath then, too.

Of course, last year he'd been partially drunk after having received the final divorce papers in the mail along with several nasty letters from creditors. His life had been at an all-time low and he'd tromped off into the woods to think. Not paying attention he'd stepped on some rotted boards on the bridge and ended up in the creek that cut across his property. He still had no recollection of how he'd dragged himself home.

"Ben?"

"Hmm?" He turned to look at Eugenie. She was damp from where he'd hugged her but seemed otherwise unaffected by their adventure.

"I asked if you were okay to drive. You've been staring out the windshield."

"Sorry." He put the car in gear and started to head for home. "I was thinking. Did I ever tell you about the time I fell in the river?"

"No."

Was it his imagination or did she seem tense? He flicked a glance at her and noticed her fingers were laced tightly together in her lap. Maybe it was a reaction to the fight. She probably wasn't used to seeing two men beating the crap out of each other. It had likely frightened her half to death. Or had it?

He frowned. At one point during his fight with Brown, hadn't he noticed Eugenie racing towards him?

"Eugenie?"

"Yes?

"During the fight, were you trying to help me?"

"Well, I wasn't going to sit in the truck and not do anything!"

"I mean, I thought I saw you running towards me and later you were yelling 'let me go!' like someone had a hold on you. Or at least that's what it sounded like. I was a bit distracted by that guy trying to stab me." He gave a dark chuckle.

"Oh. Er... There were wild vines under the snow and I got my leg tangled in one and it tripped me up. Then while I was getting up, I somehow managed to get it wrapped around me. I thought I'd never get free."

He nodded. That made sense.

"We're almost home." Eugenie pointed out the window and leaned forward as if urging the truck to move faster. "Won't it be wonderful to get inside? I want you to pop right into the bathroom and get out of those wet clothes while I make you some coffee."

She continued to babble away at such a speed he wouldn't have been able to get a word in edgewise if he'd wanted to. It was okay though. He was too busy thinking about what she'd said. *We're almost home.*

Damn, those words sounded sweet coming from her lips.

An hour later, he was warm and dry, his stomach full from the pot of stew they'd reheated. Before Eugenie had arrived in his life, he'd been surviving mostly on frozen dinners. It wasn't that he couldn't cook, it was more the fact he'd had no interest in it. Now, his freezer was stocked with nourishing leftovers and casseroles since Eugenie was always discovering some new dish she wanted to try to make.

"Come and sit by the fire with me. We can clean up later." He helped Eugenie from her chair and led her to the living room.

"Well..." She glanced back at the kitchen.

"We're both tired. It won't hurt to leave the plates on the table for once."

She conceded and soon they were seated together on the sofa, his arm around her shoulder, a fire crackling in the hearth.

"The warmth feels good," he murmured, staring into the fire.

"Are you still cold? I could get a blanket—" She started to rise and he pulled her back down.

"No. I'm fine. You don't have to fuss over me."

"But I like fussing over you."

"Well, that's kind of you but tonight all I want is you by my side while we sit here quietly."

"It *was* a tiring day."

"Yep. Battling bad guys isn't part of my daily routine."

"Thank goodness!" She leaned her head against his shoulder, one hand creeping up to rest on his chest. "I nearly had a heart attack when you left the truck to chase that Mr. Brown."

"Well, I wasn't going to let him get away. No one messes with my artwork. Especially artwork that was inspired by you."

A flush appeared on her cheeks and she lowered her eyes. "That's kind of you to say but a bit over the top."

"No, it isn't." He pressed a kiss to her forehead.

"I guess we'll have to agree to disagree on that point."

He chuckled softly and pulled her closer, resting his chin on top of her head, loving the feel of her against his side. She could protest all she wanted, but he knew the truth. She was his salvation, his guardian angel who had miraculously appeared just when he'd been losing all hope.

Lifting his gaze from the fire, he studied the portrait on the wall as he'd done so many times before. Even as a boy, the woman had fascinated him. Who'd ever have thought he'd have the real-life version in his arms?

He idly stroked Eugenie's arm, his thoughts drifting as companionable silence filled the room. What a crazy week it had been. Art shows, RCMP officers appearing on his doorstep, smuggling rings... What was going to happen to his carving of Eugenie? Would he ever get it back or would it be held as evidence for years to come? The thought saddened him but even if he never got the bust back, he'd always have the portrait and the woman at his side.

Or would he?

He frowned. How much longer would Eugenie remain in the area? There wasn't much stuff left to sort through in the shop and she'd said she moved often. The thought of her leaving created a cold feeling in the region of his heart. He should ask her to stay.

"Eugenie?"

"Hmm?"

He tried to speak but his mouth wouldn't form the words. What was wrong with him? He loved her, so it made sense that he should say it and ask her to stay. Once more he opened his mouth but then closed it again.

Coward.

That's what he was. An emotional coward. He'd laid his heart out before Sabrina and she'd stomped on it like some annoying bug. The idea of opening himself up to that kind of pain again scared the crap out of him.

But Eugenie was nothing like Sabrina. She loved him. She went out of her way to do things for him and never asked for anything in return. If he asked her to stay, he knew she'd say yes. All he had to do was man up and say the words.

He took a deep breath and turned to look at her.

She was sound asleep.

He laughed softly to himself. That's what he got for hesitating. He'd not wake her up though. She was exhausted. So was he for that matter.

Carefully, he eased out from beside her and laid her on the sofa. After ensuring the fire was safe for the night, he filled Chip's food and water bowls, then stacked the dishes as quietly as possible. For a moment, he considered doing the washing up but she might hear him. He'd take care of them in the morning instead.

Gathering Eugenie in his arms again, he carried to her to bed, flicking off the lights with his elbow as he walked through the silent house.

He set her on the bed, loosened her clothing and then tucked the blankets around her before readying himself for bed as well. When he climbed in beside her, she made a soft sound. He froze but she only rolled over and snuggled closer to him, wrapping herself around him.

With her leg over his thigh and her breasts squished to his chest, his body began to react. Making love with her would be the perfect ending to the day, a celebration of having won the fight and nabbed the bad guy. He considered kissing her awake and...

No. She was tired, exhausted if her deep breathing was anything to go by.

Instead, he contented himself with looking at her, idly twirling a lock of her hair around his finger as he took in each of her features. By the light of the moon, he studied her as she slept. So sweet, so innocent, the epitome of perfection. And she was his for the taking... if he dared.

Chapter 20

A few days later…

Ben stood up and reached for the coffee pot. "I think I'll have one more cup before I head into town."

"You're stalling." Eugenie gave him a knowing look as she gathered the plates from breakfast. "You only have two cups of coffee with breakfast. Never three."

He made a face. In just a short time she'd come to know him so well. Usually, he wouldn't consider that a problem, except for right now.

"I'm not stalling. It's more like I'm planning my strategy." He sat back down and rearranged the placement of the sugar bowl and salt shaker on the table.

"Ben." Eugenie wiped her hands on a tea towel and turned to rest her hip against the counter. "Come here."

Ruefully, he did as she asked, stopping in front of her. She placed her hands on his chest and looked up at him.

"I know you're worried about meeting with the bank manager."

"That obvious, huh?"

"Yes. I've never seen you dawdle over a meal like that. And you've changed your shirt twice this morning."

He glanced down at the blue plaid he was wearing. "Do you think the red would make a better impression? I can go—"

"No. This one is fine. Honestly, Ben, stop worrying. Just because he asked you in for a meeting doesn't mean bad news."

"I don't share your optimism." Truth be told his gut was in a knot anticipating the bank manager was going to tell him time was up and he either had to pay his debts or hand over the farm. The very idea brought a lump to his throat. It wasn't a fancy place but it had been in his family for ages, a legacy from his father and grandfather…

"I'm sure the bank manager heard the news about how you helped foil that smuggling ring and he now knows you're an up-and-coming artist. Plus, you've been able to make a few payments with the money from the furniture sales. He's probably going to offer to renegotiate the payment schedule based on the positive turn your life has taken recently." She concluded her little speech by smoothing the wrinkles from his shirt and straightening his collar. "There, all tidy and ready to go!"

He drew her close and kissed the tip of her nose. "You remind me of my mother sending me off to school."

"Your mother?" She drew back, her brows raised.

"Only in respect to your optimism. In all other ways though…" He gave a mock leer, dipped his head and gave her a very thorough kiss. By the time he was done, she was plastered to him in a very un-motherly fashion.

"Wow."

"Maybe we should go to the bedroom and finish this." He started to walk her backwards towards the hallway but she nimbly slipped from his arms.

"Nice try, Davis, but only after you get home from the bank."

"Eugenie…" He tried to pull her close again but she would have none of it.

"Nope. You need to head on out."

Chip barked at the word 'out' and padded to the door, his tail wagging.

"See?" Eugenie laughed. "Even Chip knows what you need to do."

"Fine." Grumbling, he pulled on his coat and boots.

She handed him a file of papers showing his recent furniture sales as well as images of the items that had sold stickers on them at the gallery. He didn't even remember her taking those pictures but assumed he'd been too keyed up to notice small details like that. "Don't forget to show him this proof of future income."

"I won't."

She gave him a peck on the cheek and pushed him out the door.

Standing on the back step, he squinted against the bright sun reflecting off the snow and took a deep breath. The cold winter air filled his lungs. It matched the cold dread inside him. Eugenie might have managed to put a positive spin on the call from the banker but he knew all too well that the financial world wasn't as kind and forgiving as she'd like to believe.

He jingled his keys in his pocket. Enough delaying. It was time he manned up and got the damned meeting over with. Firming his chin, he strode towards his truck.

Eugenie watched as Ben drove away. She could go with him, follow along invisibly, but knew that wouldn't be a good move. If she was wrong and the bank manager was foreclosing on Ben's farm she'd be hard pressed not to make herself known. She'd want to comfort Ben and berate the banker. No, it was better to wait here, even though not knowing what was happening would be difficult.

After she finished tidying the kitchen, she headed out to the workshop. Keeping busy would distract her from worrying about Ben and with that in mind, she threw herself into her sorting.

Some time later, she shifted one last box into place and then stood back, hands on her hips admiring her work. The back of Ben's workshop was considerably tidier and more organized than it had been when she'd first arrived. There was a pile of items for him to dispose of, things he wanted to keep were on the shelves and actual collectibles for sale were tagged and in boxes, their images posted on an online site. With any luck, they'd soon be on their way to some eager collector. Satisfaction at a job well done filled her.

In her mind's eye, she envisioned how Ben could reorganize his shop now. There'd be a display area near the front, a place at the rear for actual construction. He could even purchase one of those industrial vacuum devices that helped minimize the sawdust; he'd mentioned it to her just the other day.

"Whatchya thinking about, Babe?" Zeke appeared beside her and she gave a start.

"Zeke, you have a bad habit of sneaking up on me."

"Or maybe you're not paying attention." He laughed and gave her a wink. "I'm kidding."

She rolled her eyes. "Well, in answer to your question, I'm thinking of improvements Ben can make to his workshop. It will be some time before he has enough money to make any changes but it never hurts to plan ahead."

"True." Zeke rubbed his chin. "You know, last night I thought of a place where Ben might be able to sell his furniture."

""Really? Where?"

"The props warehouse. I should have thought of it sooner."

"Props warehouse?"

"Yeah. When a GA is on a long-term assignment they need a certain number of earthly possessions to help support the persona they created. Cars, boats, fancy furniture, the whole nine yards."

"You don't buy what you need each time?"

He shook his head. "We reuse and recycle whenever possible. Have to be environmentally responsible, you know."

She nodded. It made sense. "Ok, so where is this warehouse?"

"I'll show you, but first I have to give you this!" Zeke extended his hand and the carving appeared.

"You got it back! But how? Don't the police need it for evidence or something?"

"I did a switch and the cops have an exact duplicate so Ben can have this one. Plus, I did some memory altering, fudged a few records..." He shrugged. "The bad guys will still be brought to justice but Ben won't be involved in anyway."

"But he'll wonder—"

Zeke was shaking his head even before she could finish her thought. "Don't worry. An RCMP detective has called him and said there's enough evidence against Brown using the stuff they found in the farm house."

"And what about Ms. Standish? Will she be brought up on charges?"

Zeke shrugged. "I don't know, but I doubt it. She'll claim she sold it in good faith and had no idea it was destined for criminal activity. I wouldn't be surprised if she closes up shop and moves to a different community though. Small towns are notorious for everyone knowing everyone else's business. There are bound to be rumours."

"I hope she doesn't leave before paying Ben!" Eugenie frowned as she considered an idea. "I wonder if she could be convinced to pay Ben early."

"What are you thinking, Babe?"

"Zeke, could you and I pay her a visit? Maybe *encourage* her to pay Ben ahead of time?"

Zeke grinned and pressed a hand to his chest. "Babe, I'm so proud. That's a plan worthy of me!"

She patted his arm. "I had a good teacher."

Using angelic power, they appeared in the Maple Leaf Gallery behind a very large and hideous abstract sculpture.

"I can't believe people buy things like this," Eugenie whispered.

"It takes all kinds." Zeke replied. He straightened his collar. He was once again dressed as he'd been for the show, complete with diamond earring. "Are you ready?"

She nodded and together they stepped out into view. Ms. Standish was on the phone, her back to them. Zeke cleared his throat and the proprietress turned, her eyes widening in shock.

"I'll call you back." She hung up the phone without seeming to wait for a reply. "How did you get in here? I didn't hear the bell?" Her gaze darted to the door and then back to them.

"You must have been distracted." Eugenie shrugged. "Perhaps making another 'deal' with someone."

"I'm an art dealer. I make a number of deals." Ms. Standish folded her arms. "Why are you here? And who is this?" She flicked a look up and down Zeke. "You look familiar."

"I was at your show a few nights ago." Zeke leaned against a counter and fixed his gaze on her, offering no other information.

"Oh."

Eugenie stepped forward. "I want you to write a cheque to Ben for the items you've sold."

Ms. Standish gave a derisive sniff. "And I said I would at the end of the month."

"That won't suffice."

"Too bad." Ms. Standish moved to leave and Zeke took a step to the side blocking her path. "I..." She turned and glared at Eugenie. "What is this all about?"

Eugenie blinked innocently. "All I'm asking is for you to pay Ben what's owed him."

“No.”

“Oh. That is a shame.” Eugenie made a little moue. “I guess I’ll be on my way. By the way, did you find your panties?”

“My what?” Ms. Standish appeared confused.

“The ones that you left on the floor of your office when you and the security guard were…well…you know.” She smiled sweetly. “And you were so busy, you left your computer on with your email open. It made for some very interesting reading; how Ben’s sculpture could be hollowed out…” She let her voice trail off.

“How… I mean… You broke in…” Ms. Standish sputtered.

“The alarm didn’t go off, did it? There’s nothing on the surveillance cameras, is there?”

“Then how?”

“We have our ways.” Zeke finally spoke and took a step closer into Ms. Standish’s personal space, causing the woman to back up.

“Of course, the events of that night can remain our little secret.” Eugenie explained. “The police need never know…unless Ben doesn’t get paid of course.”

“Fine!” Ms. Standish’s cheeks were infused with red as she side-stepped Zeke and dashed off a cheque. “Here, take the money. I’m done with you and Benjamin Davis.”

“And you’d better stay ‘done’ with him. Keep your claws out of my Ben, you…you…” For the life of her she couldn’t think of a proper term.

“Bitch?” Zeke suggested.

Ms. Standish gasped. “Well, I never…”

“Oh lady, I’m sure you have,” Zeke looked her up and down. “And more than once.” He gave Eugenie a wink and then offered her his arm. “Time for us to be on our way. Have a good day, Ms. Standish.” He gave her a nod and they strolled out of the gallery, arms linked.

Once outside, Eugenie collapsed against the wall laughing. "I can't believe we did that!"

"*You* did that," Zeke corrected. "I was proud of you, how you put her in her place."

"It *was* fun," she admitted. "And Ben has his money. I'll pop it in the mail so he'll think the gallery sent it."

"Good idea."

"I hope the other artists get paid, as well." She bit her lip. "Is there a way we can share our evidence with the police without creating suspicion? If she's under investigation, she wouldn't be allowed to leave town."

"Let it go, Eugenie. As a GA, you can't always tie up every loose end. You have to trust the humans can do a few things themselves. Now let's go visit the warehouse."

With greater speed and ease than Eugenie ever thought possible, arrangements were made for a number of pieces of Ben's furniture to be purchased over the course of the next few weeks. There was also the promise of more future business as new cases sometimes require specialized items.

She and Zeke concocted a plausible story to tell Ben, and even created the necessary supporting paperwork.

"He's going to be so excited when he gets home. Not only does he have the carving back but he has work as well." She was almost bouncing on her toes, eager to share the news.

"Well then, you'd better zip back to earth because he'll probably be getting home soon." Zeke made a shooing motion with his hand. "And I need to head back to my other job."

"Okay. Thanks again, Zeke. You've been a huge help."

She waved and returned to the farm in time to see Ben pulling in.

Not sure how his meeting with the banker had gone, she crossed her fingers hoping he had good news. In the short time she'd been there, she'd come to think of the farm as home. Silly of her, since she couldn't stay forever; but if she felt that way, how must Ben feel about the place?

"Eugenie, guess what?" Ben was calling her name before the truck had stopped. From his tone, the meeting must have gone well.

Relieved, she hurried to greet him. "What?"

"I have fantastic news! The bank manager was at the art show the other night and he's friends with a well-known art dealer in Toronto. A few phone calls back and forth and, voila, I have a dealer who's going to represent me and make sure my work is seen by all the right people."

"That's wonderful!" She threw her arms around him and hugged him tight.

He returned the gesture before continuing. "And best of all, based on projected sales, the banker rearranged my payment schedule. I don't have to worry about losing the farm now."

"I'm so happy for you."

"I can't begin to describe what a relief it is." He smiled down at her and then seemed to realize they were outside and she wasn't wearing a coat. "You're going to get sick standing outside with only that thin sweater on. Get inside!" He ushered her into the house.

"I'll make us lunch and we can celebrate." She was turning to go to the kitchen when she noticed Ben shaking his head.

"Sorry, I can't stay. I only came home to tell you the news because I knew you'd be wondering. The art dealer is meeting me at the gallery in town. He's going to talk to Daphne Standish about the unsold items she has."

"Oh."   Mention of the woman momentarily dampened Eugenie's mood but she tried to hide it. "Okay. Well, you go do what you have to do and we'll talk over dinner."

"Right." He pulled her close for a hug and a kiss. "I love you. See you tonight."

"Bye!" She waved him off, a smile on her face. While she didn't like Ben meeting with the Standish woman again, he wouldn't be alone. And it was good to see him looking so happy and at ease. It was a far cry from the man she'd met a short time ago. Back then, his life had been in ruins, his attitude negative. Now he was looking forward to the future. The farm was safe, and he was going to become a famous artist, she was sure of it. And in the meantime, he had his furniture sales to keep him afloat. She laughed. She hadn't even had time to show him the paperwork from the warehouse!

She pulled the document from her pocket and set it on the kitchen table where it could be easily seen. Turning, she looked around for something to keep her busy while she waited for Ben's return. The kitchen was clean, bright and cheery so she wandered into the living room, trailing her fingers over the brightly polished wood of the mantel, then pausing to admire the painting of herself that had been done so long ago. How her life had changed from that long-ago day! Her skills as a GA were growing, she knew what true love felt like. It was so much more than she'd ever imagined possible.

Grinning at the memories, she surveyed the room. It was tidy and so was the rest of the house. Ben's workshop was organized now and... A realization hit her.

Her job was done.

Ben didn't need a guardian angel anymore. It was time for her to leave.

The smile faded from her face and she did a slow turn in the middle of the room, taking in the sofa where she and Ben had spent so many evenings, the fireplace where they'd roasted marshmallows, the carpet where they'd made love for the first time.

It was over.

Her first interactive assignment had been successfully completed.

She tried to force a smile but her mouth wouldn't cooperate. Instead her chin quivered and the back of her eyes seemed to prick. She took a deep breath and swallowed hard, pressing her hand to her aching chest.

Was it always this difficult when a case was concluded?

Fighting to maintain her composure, she pressed her lips tightly together. She had to leave but what to do? Unable to focus, she looked around distractedly as mental images of herself and Ben passed by in rapid succession.

She had to wipe Ben's memory of her, make him forget he ever loved her. Her time with him would be a vague recollection of a woman who had stopped by one day. Eventually even that would fade. He'd find another woman to love and...

A sob escaped her. Oh damn. Her hands were shaking as she tried to wipe away the tears that were streaming down her cheeks. She couldn't do it. She couldn't be the one to erase his memory.

Michael. She'd ask him to do it.

Without even worrying about the fact she didn't have an appointment, she grabbed her coat and scarf then whisked herself away to his office.

Chapter 21

The sound of raised voices outside his office had Michael looking up from his computer screen. To the best of his knowledge he had no appointments scheduled. And even if he did, there shouldn't be a commotion in the waiting room.

He stood and crossed his office, his long legs covering the distance in only a few strides then yanked open the door. Eugenie and a novice GA were standing nose to nose, their voices raised; the young man had his arms spread wide and was trying to keep Eugenie from entering.

For a moment he watched, impressed with the change in Eugenie. Just a few weeks ago, she wouldn't have had the gumption to barge in and then challenge another GA, even if that GA was a novice. Yes, she'd certainly shown growth over the course of her assignment. And, if he were correct, that case was drawing to a close which would explain her presence. Hmm, this should prove interesting.

He switched his focus to the conversation going on in front of him.

"No. The archangel is busy. He gave me the assignment of ensuring he was undisturbed." The young man's voice cracked part way through the sentence. He really was dreadfully young and much too eager, so much so that he was often underfoot. That's why he'd been given what was essentially a non-assignment. It was intended to keep him busy and out of the way until Michael was able to find someone to take him on as an apprentice.

"I have to see Michael. It's urgent!" Eugenie tried to push past the novice who stood his ground remarkably well.

Michael made a mental note of the fact before intervening. "You may let her pass."

"But you said—" The novice turned on him, then realized what he was doing and his face flushed bright red and then paled. He let his outstretched arms fall to his sides. "I...I'm sorry, sir. I didn't mean to question you."

Michael nodded. "It's all right. Why don't you go find some new reading material for the waiting room."

"Yes, sir! Of course, sir! I won't let you down, sir!" The novice saluted and scurried on his way, tripping on the hem of his gown but catching himself before falling flat on his face.

With a sigh, Michael turned to Eugenie, extending his hand to indicate she was to enter his office. "And to what do I owe the pleasure of this visit?"

"I...I've completed my assignment." She sat down in front of his desk, for once not apologizing for bothering him or waiting to be told to take a seat.

"I see." Michael took his seat on the other side. "The usual protocol for completing an assignment is to fill in a report, file it electronically and, if I have questions after reading said report, we do a face to face debriefing."

"I know. I read that...somewhere. It's just..."

"Just what?"

She clasped her hands in her lap, the knuckles showing white. "I can't do a mind wipe on Ben."

"Can't? I'm positive you were instructed on that particular skill."

"I mean I won't do it." She blinked rapidly. "I know the assignment is done, that it's time to move on but..." A tear spilled down her cheek. "I..." She looked away. "I love him."

"You love him?"

"Yes, I do and..." She swung her gaze back to him. "It hurts. My heart feels like it's breaking into pieces at the idea of him not remembering me. I know it has to be done. I know I need to let go, but..." She shook her head, her voice hitching as she struggled for control. "Can you do it, sir?" Tears were now streaming down her face.

"Is that what you really want?"

"I... No. But it has to be. There's no other option. I'm a guardian angel and... and..." She broke down completely, pulling her knees up to her chest and sobbing as she curled into a ball of misery. "I love him. I love him so much and it's killing me to know he'll not remember me, that I'll never be able to see him again."

He sighed heavily, the sight of her tears affecting him more than he'd like to admit. It hurt to love, to have to let go. It was one of the hardest parts of being a guardian angel, leaving bits of your heart behind. Especially when your heart was tender and untried like Eugenie's.

When he'd given her the assignment, he'd wondered if this would happen but knew he had to allow her the opportunity to choose her own fate. She might have been content with completing the job, merely dipping her toes into the murky waters of love before moving on. But, as he'd suspected, she'd thrown her whole self into the case, opening her heart to both the wonders and pain of love.

Eyes half-closed, he observed her grieving for the man she was about to lose. She'd been so young and sheltered when she'd died, never having had a chance to experience life. How should he deal with her? Allowing his mind to drift, he reached out to communicate with one much more knowledgeable than himself before giving a nod.

He stood and rounded the desk then hunkered down in front of Eugenie and handed her a tissue.

"Eugenie, before I do as you ask and do a mind wipe on Ben, I need you to answer one question. And I need it to be a completely honest well thought out answer so don't speak too quickly because there will be no changing your mind."

"All right." She looked up, seeming surprised to see him crouched before her. "Thank you." She took the tissue and wiped her face and nose.

"What's more important to you? Your duty as a guardian angel or Ben's heart?"

"Ben's heart." Eugenie didn't even hesitate. There'd been no pause, no sign of struggle in her countenance. She'd instinctively known the answer.

Michael nodded. Just as he'd suspected. "So, what do you think will make Ben's heart happy and whole again?"

"Me." She gasped and clapped her hand to her mouth. "I didn't mean it to sound like that. It sounds awfully self-serving. What I mean...er..."

He remained silent as she struggled to express herself. He'd not lead her to a decision by putting words in her mouth. She needed to come to the realization on her own.

"I've really messed things up now, haven't I? You're going to kick me out of the program, aren't you? I've failed." Her shoulders slumped. "And, I don't think I can work with another client. Not knowing Ben needs me."

"So, is it duty or Ben?"

She looked down, twisting the tissue she clutched in her hand then suddenly looked up, a smile slowly transforming her face. "Can't they be one and the same?"

Michael put his hand on her clasped ones, letting his warmth flow into her. "You've discerned the answer, Eugenie, as I knew you would. Your assignment isn't finished until Ben Davis' heart is whole and happy. If you were to leave him that wouldn't be the outcome."

"But, a mind wipe...?"

"Where true love is involved a mind wipe, regardless of how skillfully it is performed, will never be complete. There will always be a hole in the heart of the human left behind. A feeling like a part of them is missing."

"So…?"

"So, Eugenie, you must go back. To Ben. Be happy with him and in return he will be happy with you. You two will have a full and long life together."

Her brows knit together. "You're kicking me out of the squadron?"

"I'm not kicking you out, I am letting you go. Your wings will carry you back down to Ben's home and then they will disintegrate. Your life will be human from then on." Michael stood and moved back to lean against his desk. "It's your choice. Human or angel?"

"If it means I can be with Ben, human!"

"So be it."

Michael suddenly found his arms filled with a smiling and very feminine woman. He gingerly put his arms around her and patted her back. It had been millennia since he'd held a woman like this and the gesture felt awkward. Then, to his consternation Eugenie kissed his cheek.

"Thank you, Michael."

He felt his face grow warm and cleared his throat, gently disengaging himself from her.

"My dear," he held her at arms' length, "I merely posed the question, a higher power gave the answer. Now, off you go. You have a life waiting to be lived."

He watched as she turned to go. "Eugenie."

"Yes, Michael?" She turned at the door.

"Watch for a special delivery. A package. Oh, and one last thing, you must be truthful with Ben Davis."

"You mean, tell him about my life here?" She laughed, "he'd never believe me."

"My dear, you'd be surprised what a man in love will believe."

Michael smiled to himself as he watched her leave. He'd miss her, just as he missed Alexander. An image of the tall, blond-haired angel came to mind as he recalled the details of the events that had occurred a few years earlier. It had eventually led the guardian angel to leave the squadron.

He sighed and shook his head and returned to work. So many cases, so many humans needed the help of a good GA. He was going to be short-handed, he was sure of it. Pulling up a list of current angels under his command, he stared at the screen thinking he'd have to do some re-assigning.

Chapter 22

Eugenie appeared behind the barn, out of sight of the house and then checked her watch. Ben should be back by now and was likely working on his latest project. She hurried inside calling his name. Of course, he had no idea what had transpired between her and Michael but she felt the need for a joyous reunion even if Ben did think she was crazy. The only problem was, he wasn't in the shop.

Darn.

Well, his truck was parked in the driveway so he must be in the house. She hurried across the yard and up the back steps. Her hand was on the latch when she paused, a thought occurring to her. She'd committed to spending the rest of her life with Ben but what if that wasn't part of his plan? Yes, he'd said he loved her but was it a happily ever after love? Or passing affair kind of love?

She allowed her hand to drop to her side, insecurities bombarding her. Did he want her around on a permanent basis? Maybe he was looking forward to getting his quiet life back. Or, what if the art dealer had convinced him to move to a big city and pursue being a full-time artist? Would she fit in? She thought of Jonathan and his party and how out of place she'd felt, just like she hadn't been comfortable at the gallery a few nights ago. There was nothing fancy or special about her. Ben deserved someone he could be proud of, who could stand by his side and support him throughout his career.

Her shoulders slumped as she finally entered the house, her steps dragging. She needed to find Ben and let him go. Exactly what she'd do afterwards, she wasn't sure, but she'd not hold him back.

"Eugenie?" He turned from where he stood by the kitchen table. "I was wondering where you were."

"Hi, Ben." She forced a smile while she slipped off her coat and scarf and dropped them over the back of a chair. "I just went for a walk. Did you need me for something?"

"I just saw this order. It's fantastic. I'm glad you were here when they stopped by." He looked at the paper again before setting it down and extending his hand. "Come on, let's go sit in the living room and I'll tell you about my day."

Reluctantly she followed him, unsure she could bear sitting with him in the room where they'd shared so many happy times.

Ben sat down, leaning back with his legs stretched out comfortably in front of him. When Eugenie sat on the edge of the sofa, he tugged her backwards so she was at his side and slung his arm around her shoulder.

"I had an amazing afternoon. The art dealer from Toronto had Daphne Standish eating out of his hand. I can't believe how eager she was to make a deal with him."

"That's wonderful." She forced herself to sound enthused. "I guess you'll be moving soon."

"Moving?"

"To Toronto to pursue your new career."

He shook his head and laughed. "No way. I had my fill of the big city when I was married. Never again. At most, we'll be travelling there a few times a year."

"We?" She caught on to that one word, hardly daring to hope it meant what she thought it did.

"Well, you don't have to come along but it would be nice if you did." Ben continued talking, not seeming to notice her changing expression.

A grin spread across her face and she snuggled closer to him. He was planning on her staying! She laughed silently at her own folly. Why had she doubted his sincerity?

"I'm not going back to housing construction ever again. I wasn't cut out to run a big business but I do hope to eventually fix up this house and renovate the barn. What do you think?"

"I think it's a splendid idea."

"It's all because of you, you know. You were like my genie, making all my wishes come true."

"Um… About that. Ben, there's something I have to tell you."

She opened her mouth to explain but Chip started barking.

Ben turned to look over his shoulder out the window. "I've no idea whose car that is."

"Maybe a customer?"

"Could be." He went to check and it turned out she was correct. Ben didn't return until dinner and the rest of the evening failed to offer an opportunity to broach the topic of her being an angel. Truth be told, she didn't try very hard. One peaceful night with no worries, that was all she wanted.

The next morning Ben woke early. Contentment filled him as he listened to Eugenie's steady breathing beside him. He loved waking up next to her, loved feeling her warmth and having her scent on his pillow. Since she'd been sharing his bed, he'd slept better than he had in years.

He eased away from her, stretched and yawned planning on making breakfast for her. The room was cold and he shivered as he threw back the covers. About to swing his legs out of bed, the memory of last night's dream flicked through his mind. He'd relived the time he'd fallen in the river before, but this time Eugenie had appeared and wrapped him in warmth using her wings.

Wings?

Dreams could certainly be strange. And yet... He pulled open the drawer in the bedside table and took out an envelope. In it were several feathers, the ones he'd found caught on the edge of the door of his workshop the day he'd taken that unplanned dunking in icy water.

The feathers were pure white and softer than anything he'd ever felt. They were also larger than the feathers you'd find on any local bird. He stroked his finger along the length of one, frowning.

Angel feathers?

The fanciful thought had him shaking his head.

"Ben?" Eugenie spoke behind him, the covers rustling softly as she sat up. "What do you have there?"

"Just some feathers I found once." He turned to give her a morning kiss but she barely returned the gesture, her gaze locked on the feathers he held in his hand.

"Those are mine!"

"Yours?" He frowned. "You collect feathers?"

"No. I mean I..." She paused and ran her hand through her hair looking delightfully befuddled. "Ben," she wrenched her gaze from the feathers and looked at him wide-eyed. "I have something to tell you."

"What?"

"I...I'm an angel."

"An angel?" He blinked at her and then laughed. "It sounds like we both had similar dreams last night." He set the feathers down and stood up. "You can use the bathroom while I get breakfast ready."

"Ben, wait. I really am an angel. Or…at least I was, but now I'm not."

He stroked a finger along her cheek. "I think you're still half asleep." Still chuckling, he snagged his bathrobe and shoved his arms in the sleeves as he made his way to the kitchen.

Eugenie watched him leave then flopped back down on the bed to stare at the ceiling. That didn't go well. She had to tell him, though. The question was how, without him thinking she was crazy.

She showered, dressed and headed to the kitchen, all the while planning her strategy. Her efforts were wasted, however, for there was a knock on the door as she walked down the hallway. From her vantage point, she watched Ben open the door. Over his shoulder she saw the young GA from Michael's office.

"Eugenie?" Ben called her name.

"There's a young man here with a package for you."

She hurried to the door.

"Package from Michael. Sign here." The novice who'd tried to block her access to Michael the previous day stood in the doorway. He shoved a clipboard at her.

Quickly, she scrawled her name.

"Hmm... It seems to be correct." After examining the signature and giving her a hard look, the young man handed her the package. His hand started to rise towards his forehead as if he were going to salute her before catching himself. "Michael said he wishes you well and he'll see you again in several decades."

She glanced towards Ben who stood nearby. "Tell Michael thank you."

With a nod, the novice did a military turn on his heel and marched down the stairs.

"Who was that?"

"Umm..." She frowned. Had she ever heard the novice's name? "Just a delivery boy."

"Well, who is this Michael? I don't think I like the idea of other men sending you packages." He wrapped his arms around her and pulled her close. "You're mine and I don't like to share."

"I'm yours? Really?" Those words made her feel simultaneously weak in the knees and so filled with joy she could soar around the room.

"Of course you're mine. That is...if you want to be?" He drew back, a look of uncertainty on his face.

"Yes! I'd love nothing more!" She reached up and linked her arms around his neck, pulling him down for a kiss.

A very satisfying interlude later, Ben cleared his throat. "I have something for you." He led her to the kitchen and she saw a tiny present on her plate.

"Ben?"

"Open it."

She did as he asked, her fingers trembling. Inside the box, nestled on a bed of cotton, was a simple wooden heart, painted red and hanging on a bit of twine.

"I saw it when I was in town yesterday. It seemed appropriate given I'm a carpenter and all."

"It's lovely, Ben." She held it up and then noticed a glint of gold where the twine was attached. Was it a... She flicked a look at Ben and he nodded.

"Eugenie, will you marry me?"

Before she could reply, he continued on in a rush. "It's not fancy or anything but it was my mother's and I'd like you to have it."

"Oh Ben, it's perfect!"

His fingers were trembling as he took the ornament from her, slipped the ring from the cord and slid it onto her finger. "My father gave it to me before he died, saying he knew one day I'd find the right woman. At the time, I didn't believe him, but I guess he knew you were waiting in the wings."

Wings. She needed to tell him. "I...er...have a present of sorts for you, too." She found the package from Michael that had somehow ended up on the counter.

Ben opened it and then looked at her questioningly. "It's your birth certificate, social insurance card, passport? Why did this Michael guy have all your documents?"

"I don't quite know how to tell you this, but remember yesterday when you said I was your genie? Well, I am but not quite. And those feathers you found and kept?" She led him to the sofa and began to tell him a story about a young woman who looked after her father's files and documents at a university in England almost a century ago, a story that, of course, ended happily ever after!

Epilogue

One year later...

Zeke returned to Heaven in a total funk. His assignment had sucked big time. He hated assignments where kids got sick and died. Life was just too unfair. In the year since Eugenie had found her happy ever after he'd been slogging away helping the families of innocents. At some point, unbeknownst to him, he'd pulled the short straw and now caught every shit job out there. Did Michael have a grudge against him or something?

In frustration, he kicked the door of his locker. Honestly, he didn't know why he kept the damn thing, he had a perfectly good apartment. Habit, he supposed. He opened the door and looked at his robes and halo. Nope. They could stay there. The days when he wore those, struggling to find his place, were long gone. And, feeling as he did right now, he doubted he'd ever want to put them on again.

The door of the locker room opened and a novice GA called out to him.

"Zeke, sir, the archangel Michael wants to see you ASAP."

"Yeah? Well, I just got back and need a shower. Michael can wait."

The angel's eyes widened. "But you can't make the archangel wait, sir."

"I can and I will." Zeke slung his leather jacket over one shoulder and walked towards the exit. "Tell him I'll see him when I'm ready."

Zeke doubted Michael would kill the messenger but the novice was probably quaking in his sandals. Poor kid. He'd learn.

After a lengthy detour to his apartment, where he'd showered and had a large shot of whiskey, he made his way to Michael's office. Once upon a time, actually not that long ago really, he'd been like that novice. Now, not so much.

The door to Michael's inner sanctum opened as Zeke approached it. A show of the archangel's power that no longer fazed him.

"You wanted to see me, Michael?"

"Yes. Over an hour ago." Michael fixed him with a steely gaze.

Zeke shrugged, hooked a foot around the leg of a chair and pulled it forward before flopping down in it.

Michael's mouth tightened and he took a deep breath before speaking. "I'm glad you've made yourself comfortable. I'd offer you a drink but by the smell that wafted in with you it seems you've already indulged."

"What do you want, Michael. I'm tired."

"Yes, you've had a hard year. That's one of the reasons I summoned you. I'm giving you some time off. A vacation. You can go anywhere and do anything you want."

"Really?" He began to sit up straighter, the news brightening his spirit, and then paused. There had to be a catch. There was always a catch. "For how long?"

"You have one month and then I want you back here. I have an assignment for you."

"No more kids, Michael. Please."

Michael pursed his lips and seemed to be considering his words. "This past year, you've excelled at your job. In fact, you've become one of my most trusted GAs. The work you've undertaken has been hard but you've been diligent and more importantly you've been caring. The humans you worked with were only able to cope with their losses because of you.”

“Yeah, yeah. I’m all sunshine and light, I know.” He slumped in his chair once more.

“You’re feeling bitter.”

“How perceptive.”

“It’s not a job everyone could do. You should be proud of your success.”

“How can I be proud of escorting kids out of their human lives?”

Michael leaned back in his chair. “Would you rather they were alone and fearful? Your empathy, humour and genuineness eased the transition.”

He made a face. Yeah, someone had to do it but why was it always him? Each assignment ripped at his heart until he felt like he had nothing left to give.

“Don’t you want to know what your next assignment will be?” Michael arched a brow.

“You’re going to tell me whether I want to know or not, aren’t you?

Michael pushed a file across his desk and Zeke leaned forward to take it. He opened the folder and frowned. There was no picture. No details of a person or people.

There was just the name of a country.

“What’s this about? A bit short on information, even for you.”

“I know and I apologize.” Michael frowned and steepled his fingers before continuing. “To tell the truth, I’ve had several GAs working on this assignment, one after another. No one lasts more than a month or two. They burn out. However, you’re made of sterner stuff. I’ve tested you over the past year and I think you are the right person for this job.”

“Details, please.”

As Michael explained, Zeke felt his jaw tighten to the point his teeth ached. "You really hate my guts, don't you?" He shoved the chair back and surged to his feet.

"On the contrary, I have the utmost respect for you and care deeply for your well-being. Hence the vacation."

"Yeah. Right." With a derisive snort, he left the room without even waiting to be dismissed. Damned Michael. One month. One friggin' month before he had to face hell on earth. Well, he knew what he was going to do on his vacation. Get drunk. And then he was going to find a woman...or three!

Michael watched Zeke leave and slowly exhaled. Zeke was angry with him and had every right. It was the type of assignment no GA wanted and yet it had to be done. As the head of the squadron, he had no choice but to send the young man in; Zeke was the best GA for the job. Young, confident, capable; hopefully he wouldn't return with his spirit broken.

He slowly reached out and picked up the folder Zeke had left behind. After tapping it thoughtfully in his hand, he put it away and swivelled his chair to look out the window. The night sky greeted him, dark and endless, broken only by the glow of distant stars. Leaning his head back, he tried to relax, to lose himself in the soothing calmness of the view and forget, for just a moment, all the decisions he had to make, decisions that impacted the future of so many...

About to head off for a four-week binge of alcohol, sex and anything else that struck his fancy, Zeke took a short detour to check in on Eugenie. Helping her had been the turning point in his existence, changing him from a wide-eyed novice, like the GA in the locker room earlier, to the self-confident man he was today.

It had also ushered him into the role of an independent operative. Nor more assisting other GAs, he was on his own now and it was harder than he'd ever imagined it would be. What he'd seen and done… He shook his head. The only way to survive was to build a hard shell around himself and he hated it. He used to laugh easily, be able to kick back and relax. It felt as if his youth and innocence had been stolen from him and it left a bitterness within, a feeling of resentment towards the archangel who'd chosen the worst of all assignments for him. Damn, Michael and his smooth words about being the best GA for the job. Yeah, right.

Zeke stood outside a window watching the tableau within the house. It was a cold, crisp evening, the moonlight causing the icicles to appear like fine crystal and the snow to seem adorned with diamonds. It was the quintessential Christmas Eve, complete with the sound of carols drifting from the house and the front door bedecked with a thick green wreath. Inside the house, a tray of cookies lay on the table along with mugs of something hot that sent wisps of steam into the air, while brightly wrapped packages sat about the room.

He stepped closer, leaning one shoulder against the outer wall, curious to see what was happening. From the looks of things, Eugenie and her man were decorating a Christmas tree. Bright baubles and sparkling garlands adorned the evergreen and Ben was stretching to put a star on top. Once the job was complete, Eugenie flicked a switch and the tree lit up in a rainbow of colours.

Eugenie gave a wide smile and embraced Ben. Zeke felt his throat tighten with unfamiliar emotion. Would he ever have such a relationship with another being, human or angel? He doubted it. Zeke lifted his fingers to his lips and kissed them, then he blew in the direction of the window. With a last glance, he unfurled his wings and flew off into the night. There was a host of bottles in a bar somewhere with his name on them. And, with any luck, a woman to share them with.

Inside the cozy farmhouse, Eugenie leaned back against Ben's chest, his arms wrapped around her waist. "The painting on the wall, your sculpture of me on the mantel, a crackling fire, and a Christmas tree; it makes this room so warm and welcoming."

"I'm glad your Zeke got the carving back so quickly."

"He promised he would and when an angel makes a promise he's sworn to keep it." She looked up at the tinsel and ornaments adorning the evergreen by the hearth. "You know, I don't think I've ever seen such a beautiful Christmas tree before."

"That's what you said last year."

"Because each year the tree improves as we add more decorations." She reached out and touched the hand-carved wooden angel he'd given her a few moments earlier. "This is so lovely."

"Just like you. You'll always be my angel," he kissed her temple, "in more ways than one."

They both laughed at his reference to the secret they shared. And speaking of secrets, she had one she was dying to tell him.

"Ben, we really need to look at clearing out the back bedroom and moving all your carving things to the shop."

He turned her in his arms so he could see her face, obviously puzzled by her change of topic. "Where did that come from? It's Christmas Eve and we're decorating our tree."

"We're going to need the extra space."

"Why? The house is plenty big enough for the two of—" He stopped as understanding dawned. "Eugenie, are you...?"

"Yes." She beamed up at him. "Merry Christmas, Daddy."

He caught her in a tight hug, twirling her around and then kissing her soundly. Just as things were getting nicely heated, Chip began to bark incessantly at the door.

With a sigh, Ben set her aside. "I'd better let him out. We'll continue this when I get back. Don't move!"

As Ben headed for the kitchen, she frowned, her shoulders feeling twitchy. Her angelic senses had dulled over the months of being here on earth but sometimes she still had moments of awareness. She walked over to the window and looked outside. Everything seemed peaceful enough. Maybe it had been her imagination.

About to turn away, she caught a hint of movement, wings silhouetted against the sky. Was that Zeke? Yes, she was sure of it. But why hadn't he stopped in? She hadn't been in contact with him since leaving Heaven and hoped all was well with her old friend. Pressing her hand against the cold window pane, she whispered a message, hoping he could hear it.

"Thank you, Zeke. You helped me find my happy ending. I hope you can find yours."

Was there a hesitation in the angel's movements? Had he heard her? She hoped so. Being a GA was hard work and a few words of thanks could mean a lot. She thought for a moment and then added one final wish.

"Guard your heart, my friend."

~~FIN~~

A Message from Nicky and Jan

Hi!

Thank you for taking the time to read our story. We hope you enjoyed reading it as much as we enjoyed writing it. If so, please leave a review at your ebook retailer and feel free to send us an email. We love hearing from our readers!

What's next for us?   Well, we have our own individual stories to write, but we are considering at least two more instalments in this series so stay tuned!

Our Books

Hearts & Halos
In the Cards
Untried Hearts

Nicky Charles' Law of the Lycans series
The Mating
The Keeping
The Finding
Bonded
Betrayed: Days of the Rogue
Betrayed: Book 2 – The Road to Redemption
For the Good of All
Deceit can be Deadly
Kane: I Am Alpha

Forever In Time (standalone)

Jan Gordon
Black Silk
Life in the Shadows

Connect with us:

Email:
mailto:nicky.charles@live.ca

Visit Nicky's website:
http://www.nickycharles.com

Follow Nicky on Facebook:
https://www.facebook.com/NickyCharles/

Follow Nicky on Twitter:
https://twitter.com/nickyc_author

Sign Up for our Newsletter:
https://signup.ymlp.com/xgmsybbbgmgb

Favourite Nicky on Smashwords:
https://www.smashwords.com/profile/view/charliej

Favourite Jan on Smashwords:
https://www.smashwords.com/profile/view/JanG

Favourite Jan and Nicky on Smashwords:
https://www.smashwords.com/profile/view/JanNicky